THE EAST GERMAN POLICE GIRL

NATALIA PASTUKHOVA

BROWN
DOG
BOOKS

C000132758

First published 2022

Copyright © Natalia Pastukhova 2022

www.theeastgermanpolicegirl.com

The right of Natalia Pastukhova to be identified as the author of this work has been asserted in accordance with the Copyright, Designs & Patents Act 1988.

All rights reserved. No part of this book may be reproduced, stored in a retrieval system, or transmitted in any form or by any means, electronic, electrostatic, magnetic tape, mechanical, photocopying, recording or otherwise, without the written permission of the copyright holder.

Published under licence by Brown Dog Books and The Self-Publishing Partnership Ltd, 10b Greenway Farm, Bath Rd, Wick, nr. Bath BS30 5RL

www.selfpublishingpartnership.co.uk

ISBN printed book: 978-1-83952-500-1
ISBN e-book: 978-1-83952-501-8

Cover design by Kevin Rylands
Internal design by Andrew Easton

Printed and bound in the UK

This book is printed on FSC®certified paper

ACKNOWLEDGEMENTS

This poignant tale came to me through my grandfather,
a signals officer who was stationed near Weimar
in the fifties.

I am also deeply indebted to Peter Morris for his
scrupulous and indefatigable efforts to give my often
stilted English a more even, natural and engaging form.

PROLOGUE

Come, let me tell you a story, hard and obscure, yet of great depth.

Its origin is twofold; one, a rebuffed lover who allowed bitterness to darken his heart; and two, some fools seeking a cache of hidden gold.

But, you ask, who am I? I am a Good Spirit who keeps watch over our characters, like the Lares or Penates of a Roman household; the gods of the hearth.

Our tale is set in December 1955, in the communist state of East Germany and the hard winter of that year.

CHAPTER ONE

The hilly Thuringian Forest lay snow-bound.

By eight o'clock – an hour before curfew – on this bleak and wintry December evening, almost everyone had retired to the refuge of their poor farmsteads and hovels. Spasmodic gusts scurried over the dark and benumbed land and only the distant snorting of a goods train echoed in the stillness.

A solitary figure in baggy trousers and a thick jacket neared the railway halt at the hamlet of Edstedt, where he lingered behind a rigid snow-powdered copse of holly as the puffing grew closer.

The soot-encrusted engine, silhouetted against the white landscape, made metallic clanking sounds and expelled rasps of steam. The blaze from its fire-box reflected off the glistening rails beneath it. Its string of tarpaulined wagons clunked rhythmically over the joints in the track.

When it had gone, the boy crossed the low platform to the wooden passenger shelter. He tugged off the outer pair of his two sets of mittens, extracted a home-made poster from an inside pocket and – after fumbling with a matchbox full of drawing-pins – stuck it up.

A stencilled stylised outline of a rose preceded some amateurish ill-aligned print: 'BEFREI UNSER HEILIGES DEUTSCHLAND' – 'Free our sacred Germany'.

The lad knocked an icicle from the sagging roof, then retraced his half-obliterated boot-dents alongside a drift-submerged hedge.

In the lane which led to Essbach, his boots crunched

the chalk-like snow. He padded softly past hoar-patterned fences and rime-etched sheds. A twinkling snowman grinned.

In the slumbering crystalline town a tenuous bluish mist shrouded the wooden and stone dwellings with their dim oblongs of light.

*   *   *   *

In Essbach that same evening – Tuesday December the thirteenth – a girl drew a curtain to one side.

A power-cut had engulfed the first-floor flat, though the gas-fire emitted a wavering pinkish light.

'Kornhausgasse is in darkness too.' She noted two dead spiders strung between the inner and outer pairs of tightly closed windows. 'What shall we do? Something exciting ... or just the usual?' She spun round with a quizzical, though dimpled, grin.

Lorenz Bauss sat on the edge of the bed. She perched herself beside him and fingered a roll of blubber on the back of his broad neck.

He smiled wryly. 'Perhaps something unusual. After all that is a part of my body which seldom interests you.

How chapped your hands are.' He took and kissed them.

She shrugged. 'It's the swarf from the gear-cutting at the works. I rubbed them on your neck to smear them with fat.'

Carine could tease easily and make him tractable.

She gathered up the playing cards.

Bauss was forty-seven and stout, but energetic when

the fancy took him.

In the room were a bed, a sagging leather sofa, a coffee-table and a bookcase stuffed mostly with nineteen-thirties popular fiction. On it stood a lamp – with a dusty shade with tassels – a walnut-veneered wireless set and a pre-war telephone.

This telephone consisted of a green wooden box with a nickel-plated voice cup and an ear-piece which hung on an elevated hook. An oval brass plate read, 'Siemens & Halske – Berlin'. It had no dial as it connected only to a manual exchange.

Its hemispherical bell jangled.

Bauss rose, went to it and lifted the ear-piece.

'Connecting you.'

'Herr Oberkommissar? Jörg here.'

'Good evening, Lieutenant.'

'Sir, *Ziggi* and *Goneril* have ... '

'Stop!' Bauss cut in. 'Tell me in the morning.'

'But you said to put you in the picture ... '

'Good night!' The Police Chief replaced the ear-piece. Its weight drew down the spring-loaded hook and ended the call.

Yesterday some shifty officials from Berlin had appeared in Essbach and one was rumoured to be lurking in the town's telephone exchange. 'Party high-ups,' he bristled.

'Here?'

'Yes.'

'Doing what?'

'Heaven knows. There's a thug in a spivish suit and two snooty women.'

Bauss was Head of the Border Police unit here, the

8

Grenzpolizei. Whatever this dubious crew were up to, he dared not interfere. He had told his men though to keep an unobtrusive eye on them.

Carine lit a candle and brought in a tray with cups of coffee and two slices of bread spread with butter and treacle.

Lorenz looked glum.

She patted his puffy jowls. 'Would it please Caligula if I peeled a grape for him?'

'Reports of enemy activity. Go and investigate, Legate.'

'And leave you sulking alone in the palace?'

This pretty lass from Liège, brought cheer to Bauss. Twenty-eight and displaced by the war, she had an attractively sculpted figure, a stylish gait and eyes which twinkled, either with happiness or sadness.

The lilac nimbus from the softly hissing gas-fire shone across the fluffless threads of the carpet.

'So shall we go to bed … or shall we sit up so we're not so tired in the morning?'

Sitting in a sloppy woolly, he shook his head with silent amusement, then blew out the candle.

'Am I the light of your life, Lori?'

He nodded. 'Forty watts at least.'

'Is that enough?'

'I nodded.'

'Oh. Not just a spasm of your neck muscles?'

The town was still. The last tram had screeched by on Kornhausgasse half an hour before. He turned off the gas-fire and it faded with an orangy-crimson glow.

The hostile cold of the outside world would gradually re-enter through door-crack and window-pane, but another enemy lurked in the shadows too; a less physical one.

He had tried to hurt Isolde in lieu of her mother in revenge for those long-gone rejections, but due to some eerie mischance his plan had failed.

He chewed over half-forgotten curses. One, an archaic past participle for 'roasted', was short no doubt for, 'May she be roasted in hell.' Another, 'Blocksberg' stemmed from the saying, 'Go to Blocksberg.' This non-existent mountain was where he wished her to be entombed.

'*Au lit.*' Carine preferred to make love in her native tongue.

'*Roule ma poule,*' retorted Lorenz.

She took off her knickers, but kept on her socks, dress and woollies and they flopped into bed, pulling up all five blankets and covers. They turned to embrace blindly in their snug invisible world.

She gripped his genitals. '*Avance, s'il te plaît.*'

He stroked her hair then slid his plump fingers down onto her nicely-pointed breasts. In front of young men she would sometimes thrust them out. At least for the present though, she was his.

Carine longed to be physically loved as well as treated kindly.

After sex, he fell asleep.

She typically spent three nights a week with him and he gave her tins of food, extra clothes coupons and a little money in exchange.

After an hour she fell asleep and he awoke.

He recalled again the only girl he had truly and dearly loved. As in Plato's story of the cave, he had briefly sighted the sun, but had then been forced to withdraw to an inner darkness.

'Susanne Dettmann? My beloved Sussi?' She had sensed that elusive life-and-death force too, so why had she rebuffed him? Why?

*   *   *   *

In Essbach's only hotel, the Gasthaus Lindeneck, three rooms had been taken by the 'visitors' from Berlin.

In the poorly lit dining-room these guests ate capons, carrots and potatoes.

The sauce finally arrived.

'Thank you for being patient,' said the chef.

How do you know we're being patient? We might be seething ... ready to explode?'

He smiled uneasily and retired.

Brunhilde's father – Balthasar Axt, State Treasurer – and Luise's uncle – Minister for Harbours and Railways – had sent them here together with Edgar Joos.

On a simple street map, Joos drew a circle with a red crayon.

'Malabar Terrasse?' queried Luise.

'Yes my lovely sugar-coated bun. Number six. Where the Stehrs once lived.'

'So?'

'Tomorrow, go there please and call on a lad by the name of Thilo Hengel ... '

There were some crepuscular movements in the unlit hallway.

'Do we want the door open?' asked Joos.

'Shut it,' said Luise.

'Do you mean be quiet or close the door?'

The slinky young waitress brought in their cheese-cakes and coffees.

Joos sipped his. 'This coffee's homeopathic. "Weak" doesn't come close.'

'Do you want Turkish coffee then?'

'No I don't. I just want a decent cup of coffee.'

As she left sourly to replace their coffees, Joos closed the door. 'I asked her if she'ld spend the night with me, but was ignored.'

'Well, girls often ignore the one they want.'

'I never realised I was so popular.'

They tackled their puddings.

In West Berlin Edgar had met an agent code-named Freya on a bench beside the Landwehr Canal. Later, in the Viktoria-Luise-Platz – a once tree-caressed, attractive, turn-of-the-century oval – Freya in motorcycle gear had, in a bombed-out six-storey ruin, given him an envelope.

This bizarre escapade revolved around some allegedly missing gold from Romania.

'Does it actually exist?' queried Brunhilde.

'Well it went missing.'

'And they found two of the wooden boxes,' put in Luise.

'Herring boxes without topsies.'

'And with no herrings in them.'

'The blindness of logic, the vanity of science,' asserted Brunhilde.

'We're not all classicists,' muttered Joos.

'More's the pity.'

Up in his room, Joos recalled the newsagent's kiosk at the Schlesisches Tor U-Bahn station. There American-influenced magazines had overtly idolised the female body. No wonder girls were suddenly becoming so sure of themselves?

There was a knock on his door. It was the young waitress.

With a fist on her hip, she said, 'Twenty Marks?'

Edgar raised his brows. 'Twenty Marks? That's steep. I hope you're good?'

*   *   *   *

In her sparsely furnished garret, Greta Nagel tried to sleep.

Christoph, her new but timid boyfriend, had still shown no signs of wanting to bed her. He was a signalman, a dreamer and one who saw girls as mythological entities.

Martin, her divorced husband, had worked in a glass factory which specialised in coloured lenses for railway signal lamps. 'Cobalt gives a good blue,' he had said. 'White is the colour of safety on most lines, being brightest.'

She had once been a leader on F.D.J. camps – Free German Youth – a role which ought to have led to some privileges, but had not.

She had urged Christoph to join the S.E.D. – the Communist Party – but he had flatly refused.

Her attic room was so sub-arctic that she wore some of her day-time clothes over her night-dress and home-knitted bed-socks, under the blankets. The rusty thermometer screwed to the window frame outside, had read minus eighteen.

She had targeted Christoph in August. They were both often in the library. In an above-knee – and so very risqué – Saxe-blue dress, she had asked him about a painting there of a warship with a red flag hoisted on its main-mast. 'Does that imply mutineers?'

He studied it. 'No. It signifies "ship ammunitioning".'

She had smiled broadly. Claws can dissemble like that.

With recourse to only the simplest of pleasantries, she made it seem quite natural to go to the coffee shop together.

Yesterday she had attended an S.E.D. party, where a caucus of senior bureaucrats had puffed contraband cigars and sampled French liqueurs. Lesser acolytes, such as herself, had savoured *real* Brazilian coffee and Swiss chocolates; crumbs off the table of the mighty.

Her short brown hair poked out above the bed-clothes. She cuddled her stuffed cloth toy snake.

CHAPTER TWO

The next afternoon, as the grey tentacles of dusk touched the green-coppered domes and the cerise-tiled roofs in the sombre heart of this quaint old university town, a swaying tram rounded a curve and passed through a breach in its snow-topped medieval rampart.

Isolde rose from one of its slatted wooden seats with her basket and violin, ready to alight in the Luisenhof.

In the square the snow had been shovelled into heaps, whilst a few townsfolk, in plain unpatterned clothes, ambled in and out of the austere-looking shops; a cobbler's, a grocer's, a baker's.

She crossed over to Keplerstrasse and entered an eighteenth-century, three-storey tenement block by one of its double doors, knocking the snow off her boots on the flag-stones inside. She climbed the bowed stone stairs and with a large ancient key, let herself into one of the two top-floor flats.

It consisted of a large room with two long windows, a bathroom off and a fixed wooden ladder which led up to a low attic.

She removed her outdoor clothes and put on some plain black canvas slippers.

The elegant fireplace had been boarded up and a small iron stove stood in front of it. By raking through the ashes and adding two logs, she gradually rekindled it.

In the kitchen nook, she ran some water into an iron pot and set it to heat on the old gas hob, adding half a handful of salt from a crooked tin box.

She lit the stubby candle in the middle of the table but left the curtains undrawn, chopped up an onion and a remaining quarter cabbage and scraped them from the chopping-board into the steaming pot.

A key turned in the lock and in came her brother, who after dumping his rucksack on the battered sofa, took off his heavy snow-dusted jacket and boots. His jumper had congealed droplets of egg yolk on its back, telling that at some point it had been on back to front. He gave Isolde a smile and she smiled in return.

He extracted his purchases from the rucksack.

'Three carrots ... '

'We'll use one of those now.'

'A packet of oatmeal. Some ribs of lamb ... '

'Lamb!'

'They cost one Mark eighty. Some dried peas. Someone said the milk was sour, so I avoided that. Two kilos of potatoes ... enough cheese for a mouse-trap ... oh and the bread had run out.'

She sliced the carrot and three small potatoes, added them to the pot and stirred it, whilst Christoph set out two bent spoons, two glasses of water and two differently coloured cracked bowls from their heterogeneous collection.

'Those plumbing repairs in the basement ... the flow was the wrong way, so they put in two cross-overs, the alignment was poor and a number of joints leaked, so they inserted some S-bends ... The result's like a French horn and still the pressure's too low for Herr Goitschel's bathroom. He's complained again, but no one cares.'

Isolde ladled some of the soup into the bowls and they

sat down to eat in the flickering illumination given by the candle. They folded their hands and recited together; 'By the love of Mary, Queen of Heaven, who bore the blessed Child who died for us, we thank you for this food o Lord. Amen.'

The girl took a last crust and tore it in two, giving Christoph the larger piece. He dunked it.

'There's enough soup left for Greta.'

'She'll be here later ... I think.'

'There's a rehearsal in the Bartholomäuskirche, so you and she can be alone.'

Christoph confided dolefully, 'When I asked if she wanted to see me again, she sighed and said, "Oh, I suppose I must."'

Isolde had already sensed that this girl was not kind. 'Don't be scared by her.'

'She dreams of invites to S.E.D. parties, where everybody is *wonderful*. At her last one, the carpet had absorbed so much spilt alcohol that bubbles were fermenting under it and each time she put a foot down, it belched.'

Isolde smiled. 'It sounds *wonderful*.'

She stood up and refilled their water glasses. She wore a plain though faded dark blue skirt, a medium blue blouse and a cardigan in deep pink.

'Oh,' he began suddenly, 'a policewoman called this morning, in fact that Uta Dietl who you were at school with. She said that someone at the *Grenzpolizei* H.Q. wants to talk to us and she'll pick us up at eight o'clock tomorrow morning.'

Isolde hid her misgivings. 'Did she say what it's about?'

'I asked, but she didn't know.'

Christoph's lower lip quivered.

Isolde knew it was because of Greta. She stood up again, came round to his side of the table and pressed his head and face against her chest. She crossed her forearms behind his head and bent down to kiss the top of it. She spoke into his hair. 'Perhaps you must be brave and not see her any more?'

*　　*　　*　　*

On Wednesdays, to avoid an evening in her dreary room at the police barracks, Corporal Dietl would often visit her Aunt Monika in the village of Niederod.

When little she had fed the geese at the farmhouse, cuddled the rabbits and mended their hutches. And sat beside the kitchen fire, she could hear about who was courting who or read to her backward nephew.

By five o'clock it was already dark as she walked towards the railway station along an avenue of old mansions, in what had once been a well-to-do part of the town. Bare beech trees stood on the grass verges, which lay under snow and a thin flurry of flakes drifted slowly down, caught in the paltry glow of the cast-iron street-lamps.

A long-bonneted EMW 340, a two-litre car based on a pre-war BMW and the largest car then produced in East Germany, came into view. It bore a zed-aitch registration number. As it stopped, the girl stepped behind a tree.

Uta, if restrained with strangers, was not awkward. She had a good figure, a pretty face and dark hair. Policewomen were still quite uncommon.

A man climbed out, tall and smartly tailored. He wore a Trilby and a long crisp unbelted raincoat, almond-green and possibly from the KaDeWe Department Store in Berlin, where only the most privileged were allowed to shop.

So as not to be caught concealing herself, she resumed her walk. 'Good evening,' she said as she passed him.

The forty-year-old looked up, surprised but unperturbed. He took in her uniform and the pips on her shoulder-tabs.

'Corporal?' he called.

She stopped and turned with her right arm hanging straight down and her left hand clutching the long shoulder-strap of her handbag.

In the penumbra below his Trilby there lingered cold metallic eyes and mauve lips.

She repressed a shudder.

Joos – for this was the man's name – pinched his eyelids in undisguised carnal interest. His warrant card read, 'Staatspolizei: M.f.S.'

Uta did not know what her seniors knew, namely that in Essbach a high-ranking trio had arrived on some undisclosed mission. Her boss, Herr Bauss, suspected them to be racketeers linked to some top stratum of government. The girl did though recall a notice on the 'Orders of the Day' board. 'You are here from Berlin?'

He smiled urbanely.

Her bright bearing and curbed liveliness might lessen the drabness of his visit here? He would undo her orderly form, disinhibit her erect hour-glass poise. His genitals stiffened.

'Your name?'

'Corporal Dietl ... Sir.'

'I meant your first name.'

'Uta,' she answered guardedly.

He shook his head. 'A trifle old-fashioned?'

Her long dark hair had been wound into a bun on the back of her head, whilst tilted to the right, she wore a Prussian-blue field cap – in shape similar to a Glengarry – with a silver badge.

This fit-looking though distasteful fellow eyed her thoughtfully.

She discreetly retreated a little.

Her pale pentangular face had thin sharp brows and watchful grey eyes. Her neck was slender, her shoulders sloping but average in width and her waist narrow, whilst the broader outline of her hips clearly belied her femininity.

Her belted black leather coat had felt arcs sewn onto each sleeve, with the word 'Grenzpolizei' embroidered in white thread.

'You are not the clumsy rhinoceros which women in uniform so often are ... but youthful, agile, gazelle-like?'

A revealing cocktail dress in place of this stark regulation get-up and her hair let down would enhance her desirability even more.

'So Uta, when we can meet?'

She said nothing.

He changed topic. 'This is Ursulinenklosterweg?'

'It is.'

'A queer name, that?'

'There used to be a nunnery here, I believe.'

He nodded.

Uta belonged not to the ubiquitous *Volkspolizei*, that is the People's Police or *Vopos*, who wore mustardy-green uniforms, but to the *Grenzpolizei*. This more recondite establishment – the Border and Security Police – used a uniform based on the colour known as Prussian blue, a dark blue but not as dark as navy. Its recruits were usually of a higher calibre and with a more natural authority.

'I'm expecting a young fellow shortly, a black-marketeer.' Joos consulted his watch. 'He's very gangly ... legs like a sparrow. He sells tinned cheese which is being stolen from the District Signals depot at Oberstruttal.'

The State ran its own black market shops, the H.O. stores, to make a profit for 'the people'. 'So your purpose is to eradicate illegal competition to the H.O.?' she queried naïvely.

He waved a hand airily. 'You have the wrong end of the stick completely.' He smirked, hoping she would soon be holding one end of his stick.

She guessed his thought.

A typical wage was twenty-five Marks per week. The H.O. shops sold beef at seven Marks per pound, butter at nine Marks per pound and so forth to anyone who could afford it. This enterprise however was not apparently his prime anxiety.

Uta endeavoured to dismiss herself. 'Well, I have a train to catch in ten minutes, so good evening to you.'

'Wait Corporal. I may need your services ... ' his face brightened darkly once more.

'Will you please stop these innuendos?'

'Perhaps you're being over-cautious, Corporal?' He grinned. 'Then again, perhaps not?'

There was no one to come to her aid, yet oddly she did not feel afraid.

He eased himself back on his heels. 'I think … '

A thin youth turned in from a side-street called Malabar Terrasse and plodded toward them on their side of the road. The newcomer was poorly dressed and pulled a sledge piled with fire-wood. Joos stepped behind the broad bole of an elderly beech.

'This is him now. Step back.'

'His name's Thilo Hengel. I know him from the swimming club.' Thilo had asked her out once, long ago, simply and pathetically. She had reddened a bit and refused, since a seventeen-year-old girl could not possibly go out with a fifteen-year-old boy.

Thilo's army-style boots crunched the snow. As he drew near, Joos stepped out. 'Stop. State Police.'

Thilo jumped with fright, halted and timidly faced his enemy. *'Was ist los?'*

'Justice Commissioner Joos. Unload this sledge.'

'It's only fire-wood from … '

'Unload it!'

Thilo began tentatively to lift off odd logs and bundles of twigs, then a sudden avalanche of sticks revealed twenty or so shiny silvery metal tins. The boy froze. Joos moved up to his terrified form and out of earshot of Uta whispered, 'Well well! Pretty ham-fisted. Run for it and I'll let you escape.'

The boy hesitated, then foolishly took this deceitful advice. He burst into a clumsy sprint. With impressive speed Joos drew a pistol from an inside pocket and fired one shot which hit the youth in the middle of his back. The snow-graced silence deadened the crack. The victim fell forwards onto his front in the white powdery snow. He moved a little but could not get up.

The shocked girl ran up to the fallen form, knelt down beside him in the fresh snow and taking her gloves off, rested a warm hand gently on the back of his head. 'Thilo, I had nothing to do with this. Truly I didn't.'

Thilo looked at her sadly. 'That man's accomplice told me to ... ' he croaked. His face looked grey and a little blood started to seep out over his tongue.

She bent right down, took his head in her arms and kissed his temple. He managed a faint smile and then died. Tears ran down her cheeks.

'Discipline, if lacking, must be enforced,' muttered Joos in a low monotone.

When she did not respond, he gave her bottom a moderately forceful kick with the toe of his ornately perforated leather shoe. She gently released the body, picked up her gloves, dried her tears and stood up with a striking dignity.

His smooth-soled shoes each had two broad rubber bands with studs on to grip the snow, drawn on over them.

Joos struggled to subdue his irritation with this obtuse Corporal Dietl. Any prolonged intimacy from her supple form, should be given to him.

He put away his ugly pistol – a First World War Luger P08, Uta thought – and eyed her slowly heaving chest with a cynical smile.

She knew now that Thilo had been duped, that his death was part of a smoke-screen intended to cover up some other illegal operation.

'You didn't want him alive to question?' she stated flatly, barely keeping her tone level.

Joos watched her impassively.

They stood facing one another in the falling snow.

'A pity you are not receptive to a little licence. Life could be so much easier.'

'Or perhaps a good thing?' she snapped.

'Don't overplay your hand. I don't tolerate insolence.'

She bit her tongue.

He sighed. 'You're more staid than I imagined. Ah well, you'll learn ... ' He tried to touch her chin. 'So, when can we meet?'

She brushed his hand down and lowered her head, but the axes of her eyes focused glacially on his and her breath condensed in clouds in the cold night air.

Her coat's lapels were folded inwards and buttoned together in front of her soft white throat.

Suddenly he grasped them, bunching them in his left hand and pulling her face right up to his own. 'Who the devil do you think you are?' he growled. 'I'll screw you before I leave this town ... or else.'

His pique arose from hating her being both desirable and incorruptible. He propelled her backwards into a high brick gate-post, thrusting her against its courses of unevenly baked bricks, many burnt cinder black. Her bun of hair cushioned the bump to her head.

'So, the puppeteer tugged the strings and the puppet did not respond?' He smiled. 'Perhaps you are a glove-puppet? Though I wasn't thinking of putting a hand inside you, but something else.'

He gently pushed and pulled her back and forth and she limply let him, before he suddenly rammed her more forcefully again into the gate-post.

Two *Vopos* hove into view, whether by chance or

arrangement, Uta could not at first tell. Perhaps they were there to authenticate and deal with the corpse? Joos saw them too, but ignored them.

With a last hard thrust into the brickwork, he said, 'You are free to go … temporarily.'

The *Vopos* in their greatcoats and caps drew parallel and saluted the official from Berlin, apparently oblivious to his assaulting a police lass. Clearly they had been pre-arranged and had merely been awaiting their cue.

Uta marched shakily away.

Despite the havoc of the Second World War, most East Germans were Christian and the medieval ethics of hard work and obedience were still deeply engrained. Propriety ruled much of their lives, despite the straitened circumstances.

Joos droned instructions to the swinish and insensate *Vopos*.

The snow had stopped and the water vapour in the air was turning to fog. The soft snow, like sifted flour, stuck to the Corporal's boots as she padded unsteadily towards the station.

*   *   *   *

Spread on the table were four sheets of coarse pale-grey sugar-paper, an ink-pad, a box of large ink-stained rubber letters and a grooved block able to hold one row of type. Wearing a pair of woollen gloves, Christoph rolled up his new posters and drew a rubber band over them.

His sister, who was sorting out a sheaf of sheet music, whispered, 'Why can't you stop dabbling with this?'

'After what happened to Pappa?'

'He would tell you to throw it all in the stove.'

'Only you know about it.'

The clock on the bookshelves – which were planks separated by bricks – said twenty past six.

'Goodness. I'm late.' Isolde pulled on her boots, coat and mittens and left. Christoph turned the key in the lock behind her.

He was scrupulously careful. The paper was a kind issued to schools and the ink-pad was a widely available one composed of the standard mix of gas-black, green vitriol, and linseed oil. The pre-war *Gigant* printing set though, of three-centimetre-high Gothic majuscule letters, was rare.

He climbed the ladder to the attic and tucked these items into their hidey-holes. In this windowless roof space stood a camp-bed with a tangle of blankets on it, whilst a shirt hung on a hanger from a nail in a joist and an old tin chest served as his clothes' store.

A wooden box on its side formed a miniature stage. It had coloured cardboard backdrops and painted cut-out wooden figures of market girls and knights, sailors and priestesses. Also there lay there a collection of tools, nails and woodscrews in jars and some off-cuts of wood.

Downstairs, he removed his gloves, lit the hob with a spill lit from the stove and put the whistling kettle on.

As a clock chimed seven, Greta knocked.

He opened the door and with a sprinkling of snow on her coat she swanned in.

'On cue.'

With her coat, gloves, scarf and boots removed, she

wore a brown skirt, a stiffish cream camlet blouse, a coffee-coloured cardigan with wooden buttons and white knitted stockings.

Christoph gave her a peck on the ear, an offering which – with a lowering of her lids and an ironical arching of her brows – she permitted.

He ushered her to the well-pummelled sofa and sat beside her, but bounced straight up again as the kettle shrieked.

'Coffee?' He felt so restive.

The candle stump still burnt on the table, yet despite a shadowy and Spartan air, the room had an aura of peace about it.

Two water-colour paintings, signed 'S. Lyskirchen', hung on the back wall.

'There's some vegetable soup left for you. Perhaps goulash another day? There's no paprika, but we can manage with pepper.'

Greta languidly watched him until he landed beside her with another bounce.

She was six years older than he, sturdy and broadish in the shoulders and hips and with full breasts.

She was studying physics; such mysteries as Schrödinger's equation. With mathematics, he had never been proficient at manipulating the symbols. He had managed Latin though with a struggle.

She leant forward and drank some coffee.

Boldly, he tickled her right breast. His face was within a hand's-breadth of hers.

She stared at him.

To Greta, life was about using people, to Christoph it was about drama and writing plays and to his sister, music.

'There's an Ibsen play on, on Sunday.'

'Oh.'

'His later plays are usually based on some past crime, with everyone trying hard to behave normally and appear guiltless.' As this drew no response, he retracted his fingers. 'What are you thinking?'

She paused. 'Past crimes? My father was shot here near the end of the war … and then my mother ran off in 1945.'

'Yes. Tough I'm sure.' He touched her well-rounded right knee.

'He was with a radar section … the *Wassermann* type with the tall lattice tower.'

'Our father was shot too.'

'Yes, I know … These things make us more realistic.'

'Do they? We still have to do what seems right?'

'It changes our values.'

This inscrutable semi-girlfriend suddenly offered her soft feminine form and they kissed more intimately.

Christoph though, began to feel uneasy. Did he sense bad thoughts?

As if only she were right, she usually dismissed everyone else's instincts as rubbish.

'Come out of her you demon and go into some swine.'

'Are you the swine?'

'It's a whole herd in the Bible.'

'That's still you.' She slightly splayed her knees to hint at her willingness.

They eyed one another.

'Shall we do it?'

Her skin was lustreless and porous compared to the shiny smoothness of the policewoman's that morning; her allure far less.

'My demons are beautiful,' she whispered.

For the first time, she climbed the ladder.

Their copulating was inelegant. The camp-bed capsized instantly, but the blankets proved an adequate ground-sheet.

Her pupils were large, but her unfurled lids almost hid them.

Her arms encircled him like an anaconda. She adjusted him above her, whilst her calves and thighs manoeuvred themselves into a scissor-shape.

The mawkish flames which had licked his fiercer soul died. Was that it? That non-ecstasy? And Greta, though panting, seemed psychically quite unaffected?

'I spoke with a policewoman today.'

She pushed her heavy load upwards and inspected his face. 'That was bold of you.'

'She went to school with Isolde ... and she spends time with her handicapped nephew.'

He prised himself free and dismounted.

She sat up.

'I said she could bring him here one day to play with my toy theatre.'

With a sharp indrawing of breath, Greta clasped her hands. 'Oh, very daring!'

He ignored this. 'She seemed very sincere ... not animated perhaps, but I suppose she was on duty.'

As Greta picked up her cardigan, a button became caught between two rough floor-boards and was torn off. 'Oh, sod it!'

Christoph descended the ladder.

On her hands and knees, Greta found her button in a groove beside a tin of nuts and bolts. The shorter floorboard was loose and lifting it a little to free the button, she glimpsed the ink-pad and the tin labelled *Gigant*.

With her nails, she opened it. A thought crossed her mind. She took out a letter 'A' and slipped it into her skirt pocket.

Downstairs she sat at the kitchen table and slurped her bowl of soup.

She worked at the police station one morning and two evenings a week as a cleaner. It paid for her books and lunches at the university.

'Might I know this police lass?'

'She's *Grenzpolizei*, so possibly. Uta Dietl.'

He brought across two five-inch-high fir trees, cut out of wood and with square bits of brass plate for bases.

'For my toy theatre. When they're painted sea-green ... '

'Perhaps your new police girlfriend will like them?'

'We just spoke pleasantly for five minutes ... '

'And you misread her?'

'Misread?'

'Don't delude yourself. She'll have some tough gorilla to keep her happy.'

Christoph started to become angry. 'I simply thought she was straightforward and good-natured.'

'How charming. What must she have thought when you tried to flirt with her?'

'I didn't flirt.'

'Went all silly then and made a fool of yourself?'

'Neither of us flirted!'

'Such a temptress won't choose *you*.' She smiled. 'Or if she did, she'ld twist you round her little finger.'

He suddenly shouted. 'She's a decent lass and there'ld be something wrong with you if you didn't think that!'

'And of course, there's nothing wrong with you?' She was pleased she had annoyed him.

'I saw you talking to some fellow outside the library on Monday, yet I don't accuse you of flirting.'

'Oh, in Luziferstrasse. Perhaps it was the devil?'

'Was he giving advice or asking for it?'

She stood up, walked across and slapped him forcefully in the face. 'Go and see your waspy policewoman,' she breathed hotly in his face.

Christoph eyed her, but felt oddly pleased by his sudden intransigence.

Her Christmas card to him had been signed 'From from'. Think to care so little as to make such an error?

She bent down to put on her boots, leather ones which laced up down the front in the German style, before ostentatiously heaving on her belted well-worn coat of scuffed dark brown leather. She waited.

'Your Christmas card had no love or kisses on it. Perhaps you can't love?'

'I'm still unsure … about my feelings for you.'

'Well if you're "thinking", then you're not in love.'

'It's you who's indecisive. I keep feeling I'm being wrong-footed.'

Suddenly he felt 'decisive'.

After putting on her scarf and mittens, she lingered.

He watched her, knowing that she expected him to yield, to recant.

When he did not, she snatched up her handbag, opened the door and stalked out.

Soon after the main door had slammed shut, it opened again. It heralded Isolde's unsullied tones. 'Hullo.' She shook a powdering of snow off her coat and gave him an ironical smile. 'Well?'

'It's over.'

Isolde could not restrain a grin. 'I passed her in the square. She threw me a very theatrical sneer.'

He left off scouring the pot. 'Bread and cheese?'

Isolde picked up a pickle jar and eyed it. There appeared to be one huge pickle left. 'This looks like it would last for a month, but unfortunately it's just magnified by the vinegar and the curvature of the glass.'

'We'll divide this bit of cheese … and your monster pickle. Oh, but we've no bread?'

'There're some biscuits in the tin.' She put out two plates. 'Now we've only tomorrow morning to worry about.' She glimpsed a jar of flour-and-water paste. 'You say you're careful, but look at that stood there?'

'Don't worry. As the saying goes, "Only a genius sees what he's not looking for."'

Whilst making the coffee, he mused, 'Lovers should be kind … try to help one another, to make things natural and easy.' A distant clock chimed a quarter to nine. 'Too late for sticking up posters.'

Isolde lifted the focus of her vision to engage with his. 'Please stop. I beg you.' Her tone was soft yet earnest.

'It's all right. I feel it in my bones.' He watched her unchanging aspect.

'It is I who shall suffer in the end.'

'Never. I should confess to it and say you had no knowledge of it.'

'Where's the butter?'

*   *   *   *

Only a few passengers sat on the worn seats of the local train. Outside darkness and fog blotted out the swaying sylvan landscape.

The undauntingly direct gaze Uta had given to that *Staatspolizei* villain, still amazed her. A quiver ran down her spine.

They rattled over a girder bridge across the River Derra.

Her woolly black tights were still wet over her knees from kneeling in the snow beside Thilo. An old crone with big eyes and a potato-like nose glared at the truncheon which dangled from a strap on her left side and her pistol and holster on her right. The single-breasted coat with black buttons and no rear vents came to just below her knees. The belt was three centimetres deep and of bull-hide and had a polished brass clasp.

She alone climbed down at Niederod and set off through the semi-luminous snow. By a coppice of naked birch saplings, a fox had a rabbit in its jaws. It slunk between the cumuli of two overlapping drifts. Uta reflected that rabbits probably had an easier time in winter than foxes, safe and snug in their burrows.

Walking into the hibernating village, she noticed the misty outline of a tottering man. He lifted up a warning sign from some road works and hurled it into a field. When they drew level, she asked what he was doing. He gave her a drunken smile.

'What if a vehicle comes along and the driver doesn't

see that hole?' she queried.

He gave a raucous laugh.

'If you collapse in this lane, you'll freeze to death. Just go home.'

He started singing, so she walked away.

The farm-house loomed out of the foggy winter evening, a half-timbered building with dark red brick triangles between its heavy baulks. Alongside it were stables and a barn. In the kitchen, a decent fire burnt in the brick hearth, though fire-bricks had been placed to reduce the size of the basket and so lessen the amount of wood spent.

She changed into a slate-grey frock with a turn-over white collar and an old woolly and together with her aunt and nephew, sat at the rough table beneath the solid ceiling beams. They ate pork, mashed turnip and potatoes. Cassel pork is soaked in salty water and then lightly smoked so as to be half-way to bacon. Most farmers illicitly slaughtered a pig each November and salted it down to help them through the winter.

Uta dropped her knife and her aunt quoted the superstition that a man would visit her. In local folk-lore, dropping a knife signified that a man would call, a fork a woman and a spoon a child.

Above the table hung an oil-lamp. Aunt Monika talked of pre-war days, of plentiful ground coffee and grey bread with unusual cheeses and apple cake and cream, of home woods not over-cut for fuel, hard work and general prosperity. At Uta's christening there had followed party tricks and speeches recited from Schiller.

Then in August 1939 streaks of a vivid red in the western sky had been seen to flow eastwards. This had been interpreted as an inferno of war which would start in the West, but move to the East.

Uta read to her nephew Iddo in the halo of light thrown out by the fire.

'By the quiet fireside in wintertime,
When castle and farm lay deep in snow ... '

And she talked about the pictures in the book. *'Was ist das?'* she would say, pointing to a tree say in one of the coloured drawings.

Iddo was nine but mentally four.

When he had gone to bed, Uta sat unravelling an old black pullover and then looping the twisted wool into skeins ready for darning her tights when necessary. Aunt Monika boiled the coffee-pot and talked about her current hardship.

Yet Uta was sceptical. Aunt Monika was plump and her smiles seemed neither overly authentic or kind. Uta had glimpsed her ration book once and it was a grade above the level usual for a small-holder. There were also chocolate bars in the cupboard, tokens for trains and vouchers for shoes. Also she possessed a telephone – an uncommon item – with its glass Leclanché cell which had to be filled up with sticky messy salammoniac fetched from the post-office periodically.

Uta guessed she were an informer.

Her antipathetical opinions too were both myopic and unattractive.

After a second cup of chicory-flavoured coffee substitute, Uta went to bed in the narrow cot in the downstairs back-room.

A faded photograph of her grandfather smiled from a

neat Lalique glass frame. He had lived nearby and been a woodcutter, fit till the day he died at eighty-three. He had been upright, kind and with a disposition shaped by the seasons. He had been the last living soul who had sincerely loved her.

She dreamt she were resitting her police driving test in an ageing lorry with a heavy left-sided hand-brake and a hand throttle. The examiner asked, 'What does that church clock say there?'

'Don't know. Can't see it, Sir.' She had kept her eyes firmly on the road.

A drunkard slung a warning sign with an outline of a fox on it through the windscreen.

Then in the prism of her subconscious, she saw Thilo's waxen features.

Their priest's last homily had compared Saul, whose wicked plans led nowhere, to David for whom everything had fallen into place.

The alarm clock buzzed. Four twenty. Time to get up. Time to be the daytime Uta, practical and well-disposed, a balm in a troubled land.

CHAPTER THREE

The previous autumn, Ministers Axt and Stege and the latter's niece Luise, dressed as ramblers, had climbed to an isolated mountain hut.

They had long since outgrown the juvenile game of trying to appear virtuous by expressing in-vogue opinions.

'Goats don't eavesdrop.'

'So, "The nine bright shiners".'

'Or forty, even?'

'History. The Romanian National Bank sent its gold to Russia in 1916, for safe-keeping.'

'A risky move.'

'Indeed, as Moscow then claimed that the cost of armaments supplied had exceeded the deposit's worth.'

'So come 1920, their treasury was empty?'

'Not even a ruble down the back of the sofa.'

'But with their Transylvanian mines at Rosia Montana – active since Roman times and with the thickest gold-bearing veins in Europe – and with the cereals and oil imported by Germany being paid for in gold, their reserves gradually rose again.'

'Now our key player is a Colonel Erwin Stehr … '

A goat nudged the door open.

'Good afternoon, Billy.'

'He's smelt our picnic.'

'Shall we break to eat?' suggested Stege.

Luise unpacked the haversack.

'Stehr,' she sighed, 'there's a name. I knew a *Wehrmacht*

lieutenant named Stehr at St. Lô ... Eighty-four Corps Signals. We acted in a Christmas play together ... I as a Brittany peasant girl, clad in a flutter of bright rags.' Her rose-tinted thoughts floated back to those strange wartime days. 'We were quartered in a tumble-down farmhouse ... but he had a wife back in the Ruhr.'

The men chewed their bread and sausage and smiled at her reminiscences.

'He bought me gifts though ... which pleased me.'

'Very feminine ... to like gifts I mean.'

They toasted their futures with the half-bottle of champagne.

Stege said, 'When I was little, we had three geese which slept on a peninsula in the lake. One day they squawked loudly and we found the dead body of one by a holm oak and – following some feathers – its head. Foxes it is said though, are clever enough to leave a trail which leads away from their den.

The wooden boxes found near that mine just north of Rohrdorf, the Russians concluded were a decoy.'

Axt also made a detour. 'The gold ingots held by central banks, weigh four hundred Troy ounces ... in metric, that's twelve point four kilograms. They are cast with a foundry mark and a year and are of at least ninety-nine point five per cent purity ... then stamped with a serial number.'

Luise had barely eaten as she wanted to be more shapely in order to find a lover.

*   *   *   *

A grey saloon with black mudguards and running boards and a 'Polizei' sign above its flat windscreen, rumbled along between the workshops and chimneys of Essbach.

On the back seat sat Christoph and Isolde Lyskirchen.

'So you are not arresting us?' probed Christoph.

'No,' answered Corporal Dietl.

The summons was too civil for it to be about the posters.

Isolde asked, 'When we left the High School, did you not go into ballet?'

'Yes, a year in Kiev and Moscow … but I didn't make the grade.' After a silence she added, 'At least my joints won't be worn out before I'm thirty.'

'I remember you too in that play, *The Knave of Hearts.*'

Uta was silent.

'And being very pretty,' Christoph injected. Uta smiled laconically, so he added, 'Is that the best line I've said so far?'

'I thought it was rubbish.'

'True, but it's still quite good.'

The snow-chains made a low drubbing sound.

'It's the Chief himself who wishes to see you. He was bathing his dog in the basement earlier, but he should be free by now.'

'Who uses the water first, him or the dog?' He saw in the mirror that the policegirl attempted a frown, though her cheeks dimpled.

Through the frost-edged window, Christoph glimpsed a warehouse where he had once worked. Under a projecting canopy a lorry was being loaded.

'Herr Bauss is usually fair-minded, so I suggest you don't bait him.'

They juddered over a level-crossing, then swerved into

the driveway of a former château. Set in a snow-covered park, it was the local headquarters of the *Grenzpolizei* – the Border and Security Police – who as opposed to the *Volkspolizei* had border surveillance, counter-espionage and anti-subversion functions.

They halted on the rutted ice of the motor transport square beside a grey lorry with a black awning over its cargo space.

The threesome alighted in the thin chilly haze and walked to the main entrance, where Private Baumeister with a sub-machine-gun, stood on sentry-go in a blue fur-collared greatcoat. They ascended the three wide stone steps to enter the high entrance hall through its walnut and glass swing doors.

After Isolde and Christoph had written their names in the visitors' register, which lay open on an inlaid rococo table, Uta shepherded her charges via a magnificent curved carved staircase, up to the first floor.

Christoph lingered to study a large fading canvas of a troop of Upper Palatine cavalry. He pointed to the Latin inscription. 'Do you think anyone here can read that?'

In a restrained voice, Isolde said, 'Let's just worry about this meeting. Be polite … and don't treat it like a game of poker.'

Christoph whispered, 'Bauss had something to do with father's death.'

'And I suspect with Mamma.'

A large door with cream gilt-edged panels bore a wooden plaque; 'L. BAUSS – OBERKOMMISSAR'.

Uta stood sideways on to the door, removed her gloves and knocked.

She gave the brother and sister a reassuring smile.

*   *   *   *

Greta walked past the gas works in Steinwiesstrasse. Footprints in the layer of fresh snow marked the pavement. She halted at the closed level-crossing gate together with a lorry and waited for the eight ten to Stonna to pass through. A poster stuck on a telegraph pole had been mostly torn off, but ' … UTSCHLAND' remained.

Discreetly she took the letter 'A' out of her handbag and held it up. It matched.

With a whoop from its whistle, a soot-caked Borsig tank-engine and a carriage clanked by, emitting soft regular hisses.

A signal on a tall lattice mast clanged down.

The crossing-keeper opened the gates and Greta resumed her short journey to the *Grenzpolizei* H.Q., her place of part-time work.

*   *   *   *

Bauss put his newspaper to one side.

'Come in.'

The winsome Corporal Dietl entered, came to attention and executed a salute. 'Good morning Herr Oberkommissar. Christoph and Isolde Lyskirchen are here.'

'Oh … er, show them in.'

His office was quite grand. A square of thick pink carpet on a parquet floor supported a large heavy desk under a stuccoed ceiling, while the long windows were edged with dusky blue floor-length curtains tied back with tasselled cords. Goethe could have sat there with a quill, ink-well and a bottle of gum arabic, writing up his impressions of Venice.

Bauss's uniform shirt had bronze crossed cannons on its epaulette slides and a red lanyard round its left shoulder. Exuding an ambiguous smile, he waved his visitors to chairs on the opposite side of his desk.

Uta left, closing the door gently.

Christoph took a seat and opened his jacket with its frayed collar. Bauss sensed the introspection of youth, yet had it been his own son, he would surely have found delight in him.

Isolde was in a higher sphere. Her shiny face had slightly lowered eyelids – either natural or habitual – whilst her curtailed smile just revealed her even white teeth. She took off her mittens.

'So Isolde and Christoph, I wish to talk to you about the death of your father.' The Police Chief took on a business-like demeanour.

Isolde acknowledged his words with a tilt of her head.

'Firstly, your father's life? Correct me if any of this is flawed.' He picked up a sheet of paper. 'Ekkehard Lyskirchen. Born Munich 1905. Electronics engineer. 1930 married Susanne Dettmann, a trainee nurse from Innsbruck.' Here he swallowed and his Adam's apple bobbed upwards. 'Children born 1931 and 1935. 1933 moved to Cuxhaven ... naval range finder design ... In 1938 Freiburg, before the war took him to Leipzig to work on nuclear isotope separation ... yes?'

He paused.

Where was this leading? Isolde suspected that somewhere here lay a long-lost element of rivalry or antagonism.

'The war's end found both him and you in the East, whilst Susanne was still in Freiburg.' He knitted his brow.

Oh, his beloved Susanne, who had married this misplaced nobody, this impostor. Only loving her unceasingly could bring him peace.

She had come east to join them in 1946. Because she loved her husband? No, in italics. Perhaps for the children?

'So why did your father suddenly involve himself in this foolish pro-western subterfuge?'

'What "pro-western subterfuge"?' queried the daughter.

'Betraying scientific secrets.'

'We don't believe he did,' Christoph interposed. His eyes probed Bauss's. The Chief of Police glanced evasively upwards.

'He had no strong political leanings ... and was always truthful,' said Isolde. 'And our mother now lives alone in some backwater on the Baltic coast.'

'I believe that was her own choice?' Bauss fought an involuntary tremor. Had she told them why? No.

Isolde eyed him diffidently; even perhaps with sorrow.

'Your father though ... he knew the restrictions here?'

The children seemed unable to formulate a response.

'I understand you're both religious?'

They nodded soberly.

'Austerity and hardship create character.' A trial smile flickered across the Police Chief's baggy face. 'The wish for individual stature, sadly, is a half the lure of sin.'

Isolde lowered her head.

'It is a manifestation of arrogance.'

'And the other half?' Christoph asked with a hint of irony.

Bauss fumbled. 'The temptations which follow on from being unloved?'

'Aren't they the same?' asked the girl.

He shook his head and slurped his coffee.

Christoph asked, 'He was arrested at the bus-stop in Sonndorf?'

Bauss met the boy's rapt expression. 'Yes.' He suppressed a cruel smile.

Isolde touched her forehead onto her backwardly-sloping finger-tips.

Christoph had borrowed a bike and cycled there, a spot with an iron bench surrounded by bluebells. Rooks had squawked overhead.

Isolde's eyes were a translucent blue, her face pale yet unspoilt. Her fairish hair was woven into a short plait bound with a piece of blue ribbon.

She thought, 'You have asked us here to study us.'

Lorenz did not flinch. Yet the pain he had suffered? He had struggled to live a true life despite his burden. And the inflicter of his suffering – the one who should have given her love to him – did she not bear a share in his shortcomings? If he was not his true self, the good or white Lorenz, was she not an accessory to this failure?

He pressed the pads of his two sets of fingers together. 'Anyhow the point of this meeting is to say that I shall not disrupt your affairs provided that you behave.'

'Does that mean, "Do not ask awkward questions"?'

'We are not bitter,' put in Isolde.

Her aura though seemed to say, 'I am truer than you and could heal you if only you would stoop down.'

He padded his brow. She did not appear to have recognised him.

'So, that's it. Good day to you.'

He refolded his newspaper, but it did not fold neatly. 'Let us hope this is not your parachute, eh Christoph?'

Isolde stood up. 'Thank you for seeing us Herr Oberkommissar.'

Outside in blouse tie and skirt, Corporal Dietl waited for them. She escorted them to the canteen and brought each a glass of hot milk and half a roll with a thin slice of Rosette-de-Lyon sausage and tomato on it.

'At least we've seen what he looks like,' Christoph muttered to his sister.

'Yes.' Then she remembered; Ebbkirch in 1945.

*   *   *   *

One floor down, in a bare cream-painted corridor, whose sole adornments were faceless grey doors and a notice-board, Greta in a belted smock and apron scrubbed the floor, kneeling on a rubber kneeling-mat and using a wooden scrubbing-brush, a block of soap and a pail of warm water tinged with disinfectant.

She reversed a yard at a time, but at one point, arching herself backwards because of her aching back, found herself alongside the notice-board. Amongst its dreary official memoranda, her eye caught sight again of one of Christoph's posters and scrawled across it in red, *Wer hat dieses Plakat gemacht?*: Who made this poster?

She heard footsteps and resumed her scrubbing.

Udo Eckman in grey flannels, white shirt and a plain tie and clutching some papers in order to look busy, approached Greta from behind. With narrowed eyes he surveyed her bulbous form, stopped to throw open a door and disappeared into that room. Its wooden sign read, 'Rittmeister U. Eckman und Leutnant G. Niehaus'.

Inside this cramped office, in which the peripheral floor space not occupied by the table had squeezed into it a coat-stand, three chairs and three filing-cabinets, he sat down before leaning over to his colleague Jörg, who in shirt-sleeve order was engaged in playing battleships on his blotter with paper-clips. He said in a muted voice, 'Who's that wench scrubbing the floor?' He jabbed a thumb at the door.

Jörg looked briefly puzzled. 'Oh, she's a student ... Sabrina I think her name is.' After a moment he added, 'Do you fancy her?'

Eckman beetled his brows and nodded.

'Sturdy though, isn't she?'

'But sexy. I bet things happen there in the middle of the night.'

'She looks a bit sour.' He paused. 'Probably give you hell.'

'I don't intend to marry her. I shall kick her out as soon as it's over.'

The Lieutenant changed the subject. 'His Lordship came in yesterday with this "communiqué" from the local Party magi. He wants us numbskulls to redouble our efforts to find the spoil-sport who's sticking up these things.' He waved a hand at yet another of the 'Befrei Deutschland' posters which was gracing the cork pin-board on their office wall.

'We know it's someone who can't sleep at night.'

'Someone who can't catch his Sabrina?'

'If he had a vibrant girl, he wouldn't be pissing about at this lark.'

Jörg adopted a conspiratorial tone. 'I thought you were fishing for Uta?'

Udo gave a regretful shake of the head. 'I didn't sense the green light … and it's bad for my ego to be refused.'

'At least she quickens our pulses.'

'You give her a shot. You can be the infantry and when she's exhausted from mowing you down, I'll come in with my tanks.'

'Puh! According to you, she would by now be lying face-down on her bed, pounding the pillow with her fists in feverish anticipation.'

'Well … even Napoleon had the odd set-back.' His bushy moustache twitched.

'And what about that Russian girl you chased after?'

'Russian girlfriends one, will never pay for anything, even if they have means and two, they demand extreme virility.'

'So is that why you gave up?'

'Ho ho ho.'

Niehaus smiled softly. 'Viktoria on the switchboard's nice … and is "unused capacity".'

'But she'll be wanting marriage … family?'

'I don't see that as an obstacle.'

Niehaus rose, perched himself on the edge of the desk and lit cigarettes for them both. 'Right, these posters? We need to show a modicum of activity. What can we do apart from wait for a lucky sighting or an informant's tip-off?'

The Captain leant back. 'Take notes.'

The Lieutenant sat down again, found a pencil and paper and cleared a space amongst the coffee cups and paper-clips.

'One: plot all known poster locations on a map together with dates ... actually, I've an inkling that they're all on or near railway premises? Two: find out what this emblem is on the top of the posters.' Here he stabbed at the printed rose with a nicotine-stained digit. 'Three: signal to ... '

'Well it's a rose.'

'I can see it's a rose, but what does it mean? Three: send a despatch to ...'

'During the war, some anti-Nazi Germans used a white rose as their badge.' Niehaus stubbed out his cigarette butt.

'Right. I didn't know that. I'll pop along to the archives in a bit and see what I can unearth.'

'Plenty of nooks and crevices there ... take the insipid Sabrina along ... and chat her up.'

'She'll look a lot less insipid when I've finished with her.'

'Perhaps her last boyfriend was a flop. Perhaps that's why she's so crabby?'

Eckman gave a short harsh laugh, then rapped the poster again with a knuckle. 'Three: offer a reward. Four: send a memo to Sunray. Five: have a couple of plain clothes men out each evening to stop anyone who has no obvious purpose ... ' He paused as his well of ideas dried up. 'Jörg, fetch a map from the stores and start plotting!'

The Lieutenant scribbled leisurely.

'No time like the present.'

Jörg looked surprised. 'What, now?'

Udo clapped him on the shoulder, 'This instant. Take a specimen to our codicological expert too. See what he can come up with.' Eckman winked. 'Come on man, don't tarry … and take your time … ' He sucked air in through clenched teeth, flexed his right arm and palpated its biceps muscle with his other hand.

Finally the penny dropped and Jörg left while the Captain made shooing gestures behind his back.

After his assistant had gone, he straightened his tie and gave his shoes a quick wipe with a duster, then he re-opened the door and peered along the corridor. Greta was still scrubbing, but had now receded some way. This time he saw her from the front. Apart from the plain blue short-sleeved dress, she wore a hemp apron of a weave so coarse you could see the individual threads. No one else was about, so he stepped out, walked casually up to her, bent down and placed his two forefingers into the dimples in her cheeks. She jerked backwards into the upright kneeling position and looked startled.

He gave her a disarming smile.

'Yes?'

'Sabrina?'

'*Greta*,' she said rather stand-offishly.

'Greta! I'm sorry. Misinformation from some moron who does not appreciate your loveliness,' he said with patient indulgence. 'I've knocked some coffee over and its run onto my office floor … would you do the honours?'

Unsure what was afoot, but with an inkling that it might

not be spilt coffee, she stood up and complied. Wearing a slight question mark on her face, she followed him in with her bucket and floor-cloth and he closed the door softly behind her.

'I'm Captain Udo Eckman. I hear you're a student, Greta?'

'Yes. I read physics at the University.' She saw the twinkle in his eye and a restrained smile forced itself onto her features. She even went a bit red and bashful and it made her unusually appealing.

He laughed. They both knew what they were about; so easy. 'I'm sure you look even prettier when you're not wearing this piece of sacking?'

'What can I do for you, Captain?' Her eyes looked up at his and she forged a broader grin.

'Do you suspect me of ulterior motives?'

She rocked her head non-committally from side to side.

'Do you *hope* I have ulterior motives?'

'It depends how ulterior.'

She said this very matter-of-factly and he laughed. 'No, the truth is that you've been keeping me awake at night for the past week. That's a grave offence.' He hesitated so as to make it all seem a bit more spontaneous and uncalculated. 'May I ask you out … today?' He ended with a hint of urgency.

She looked down at her bucket and her face grew more serious. 'What do you mean exactly?'

With a great display of earnest, he said in his strong Saxon dialect, 'Greta … I should go to the red light district if that was all I wanted!' This sounded contrived in contrast to his initial well-executed sallies, as soliciting a prostitute involved risk. 'I've some theatre tickets … for the ballet *Giselle*,' he urged with a persuasive grin.

She looked at his nasty little moustache for a few seconds, trying to decide. 'The difficulty is … ' she began.

'You are *so* feminine.' He held his arms out in a crooked position, like a crab eager to embrace her.

' … that I already have a boyfriend … though nothing happens beyond false starts.' Although Christoph had clearly ditched her, she had no wish to make it too easy, even for a police captain. The ballet though sounded good.

'Some pimply nervous youth, I surmise?' Udo displayed both distaste and commiseration. 'Has he started shaving yet?'

'He keeps cutting himself. I think he's shaving against the grain.'

'So his head's wooden?'

'Definitely.' She was buying time. These were perilous waters.

'Greta, it's clear that you shouldn't embark on such an enterprise lightly, but I have a real tingle … ' Enacting a rigidly poker-faced passion, he breathed, 'Come to the ballet. If it doesn't click, well we've still had a nice evening?'

She wavered. Her vanity led her on whilst a vestige of instinct uttered a muffled warning. 'Can I give you my answer in the canteen at lunch-time? If I nod my head, then tell me the time and the place.' She picked up her bucket.

He winked roguishly.

With one hand gently touching her shoulder, he ushered her out with a flourish of well-acted smiles.

After he had closed the door, he rubbed his hands and a lushly wrinkled grin suffused his face.

*　　*　　*　　*

Bauss perused. 'Isolde Lyskirchen. Reads music at the University. Scholarship grant awarded August 1952.' Quite an achievement that for someone never in the F.D.J. Christoph had attended the Lyzeum, then unsuccessfully sought a place at the School of Dramatic Art. He worked on the railway as a signalman. Not such a hard job ... plenty of time to study ... and to think. Too much perhaps? And the flat they shared in Keplerstrasse was central, quite large ... especially now that there were only two of them.

He stood up, walked to the window and gazed out at the arena of disturbed snow and the row of vehicles lined up in the middle distance.

If even at this eleventh hour, Susanne were to come to him, his *ego malus* would dissolve instantly.

In his comfy chair, he dozed off.

Isolde appeared, her tones pithy if soft.

'Lorenz, you are an ingenious spider, able to spin three-dimensional webs?'

'Isolde? It did not begin like this.'

'But now you are trapped inside one of them?'

'I tried so hard to win your mother ... but she was purposely illusive; immune to my every strategy.'

'But now? *Quo vadis*, Lorenz?'

'If now I am bad, are there not gradations of wickedness ... as of virtue?'

She did not reply.

'Abstract perfection – as with the musical scale of E major or a binomial equation say – may exist, but that is not the nature of human affection.'

The gun-ports of her eye-sockets narrowed.

'I tried to flee to Switzerland … but I couldn't obtain an exit visa.'

'I'm surprised they refused *you* an exit visa?'

Suddenly he despised her condescension, her dulciloquy. 'You fraud. You tormentor. You daughter of Susanne. I detest you.'

'So will you spill my blood on your nice pink carpet?'

The telephone jingled.

*   *   *   *

On the way to a lecture, Greta called in on her grandmother. The diminutive brick terrace-house had stone-hewn doorposts and lintels all painted cream.

The dim drab parlour had a single north-facing window, whose aperture was narrowed by damask drapes and with a light influx further impeded by lace curtains. The pendulum of a grandfather clock ticked irritatingly.

Her grandmother wore a shapeless thick cardigan over a green dress, which stopped short of the varicose veins coursing tortuously over her ankles.

On the coffee-table, on a Christmas runner cross-stitched with the three kings, the hostess placed a china coffee-pot and an ornate plate of wafer biscuits.

'How are things with Christoph?'

'I've stopped seeing him.'

'His father you said, was executed for treason?'

'He and his sister sold some paintings to raise *eighty* Marks for a small headstone.'

'On the last night of his leave in forty-three, your father sat up all night making a model crane. I've kept it ever since.'

Greta had heard this many times before.

'There's an Italian cook-book too, which he brought home from the farmhouse he was billeted in in Umbria.'

'So we can make macaroni cheese?'

The grandmother rocked a little in her rocking chair. 'Do you ever see Eitel?'

Eitel had been Greta's teenage sweetheart. She shook her head.

On the dresser a faded photograph showed a family group; women in crinoline dresses, men in baggy suits – one with a cigar, a second a preacher with a solemn aspect – and a military fellow in his cuirass, Hessians and Pickelhaube.

'Eitel was a good boy.'

The girl cast a faint smile at the grey bun and wizened eyelids. 'Grandma … the world's changing.'

'Life may be less refined, but we all need to be with the right man.'

Greta looked up at a painting in a gilded frame, depicting Italian peasant girls picking blackcurrants.

'Your Great-Uncle Gottlieb served as a gunnery officer in the Austro-Hungarian navy. Carolina, his wife, painted it. They had a villa near Trieste.'

Greta poured the coffee, added cream and sugar and stirred both their cups.

'It's a topsy-turvy world today.'

Greta gave her a lop-sided smile.

'Do you have a new man?'

Greta flushed. She had no girlfriends to speak of.

A plainer photograph showed a *Wehrmacht* officer in his late thirties. This was her father.

'When he returned from the failed Iraq campaign in forty-one, he was shrivelled and with a yellow face. Someone asked, "Have you come from Tibet?" He had lost weight and caught malaria. At home on leave, he had a relapse and we had to put him in a bath of cold water and add snow to it, until his rigors settled.'

'So he survived that, only to die at the hands of fellow Germans?'

'Yes … trying to give us a brighter future.'

'They all thought that.'

'This was different.'

'Is there anything you would like for a Christmas box, Grandma?'

'Another light bulb would be nice.' She had only one which worked and it had to be moved from room to room.

Greta left, marching purposefully through the snow, the low rays of the sun shining on her round comely face.

The heels of her boots rang out on the granite cobbles where the snow had been cleared. After the lecture, she would revisit the police station, accept Udo's offer, then go home and dress for the ballet … and for action.

* * * *

Bauss returned from a meeting with Herr Sieber, a nasty little S.E.D. official, regarding some unrest in a nut and bolt factory.

He closed the door, tripped on the edge of his pink carpet, stumbled forwards and hit his head on the corner of his desk.

With blood trickling down his temple, he extracted a handkerchief from a trouser pocket to stem the oozing and sat down.

Then, whilst shuffling some papers on his desk, he upset a coffee cup. Some flecked cold fluid flowed out onto a bound document. Angrily he swore and lashed the cup with a handy baton, breaking it but also upsetting the ink-pot. He watched helplessly as marine tentacles spread across more papers.

Was this sleight-of-hand Isolde's doing or was he simply paranoid?

He turned the rotary switch beside the telephone to two – it had seven possible positions – and lifted the ear-piece. This internal automatic exchange had been installed by the last Landgrave in 1927. 'Send up Corporal Dietl.'

Despair gripped him. He was too old to get away with such outbursts.

Uta knocked and entered. She had no hat on, so did not salute. Her eyes widened.

'Tidy it up.'

She disappeared and returned with some cloths.

As she dabbed and blotted deftly, he took in her slender neck, the outlines of her dainty shoulders and her narrow indented waist – barely wider than his cap it appeared – where pale-blue blouse met dark-blue skirt.

'Uta, if you fell in love with someone you disliked, what would you do?'

She looked up. 'I suppose it would depend on how strongly I felt?'

'Hmm.'

'I knew of someone to whom this happened. She despised the fellow by all accounts, yet also felt very much drawn to him.'

'So what did she do?'

'She made herself impossible ... and obnoxious.'

'And did it work?'

'Well she married someone else.'

'But supposing this fellow absolutely refused to be shaken off ... would that not tether her in some way?'

'I don't know, Sir. I've no experience of such things.'

'*Operation Maria*' stood out, hand-written on a file. A note clipped to it read, 'Ziggi = E. Joos, Goneril = L. Stege ... '

'Sir, does this refer to those M.f.S. agents from Berlin?'

'This file does not exist. Do you understand?'

She summarised her encounter in Ursulinenklosterweg.

He listened whilst inspecting his handkerchief. The bleeding had stopped.

'Why are they here?'

'I wish I knew. Keep your ears open.'

She threw the broken fragments of china into the waste bin.

'If you feel threatened, stay here ... and out of sight.'

'Thank you, Sir.'

He smiled. 'We like having you around Uta ... you jolly us up a bit.'

As she gave a watery smile, the telephone rang.

Covering the mouthpiece, she said, 'It's Herr Sieber ... '

'Whatever it is, tell him I couldn't care less.'

Uta removed her hand. 'Herr Bauss is busy just now.'

She picked up the stained towels.

'Christoph Lyskirchen ... he works as a railway signalman at the Rohrdorf box?'

'Yes, Sir.'

'I want you to go there this afternoon.'

'He's not on duty today.'

'No, I know. Pop along and ask whoever *is* there for a copy of their rota.'

'On what pretext?'

'You don't need one ... it's police prerogative.'

She exited.

Bauss had spoken to Uta as if she were his daughter, confident of a sensible new angle on any knotty dilemma. She was a good lass and she understood that favours and respect had to be earned.

Yet even she would be unable to unpick his Isolde conundrum; the girl who taunted him under a charade of meekness; a cloak of perilous, piquant woad-woven quietude. No one had the wisdom to unlock such mystical arts. Everyone would just slobber like piglets ... and feed him hips and haws.

Oh for someone to defile her, to tousle her pubic hair, to rub her vulva, to chafe her labia.

CHAPTER FOUR

'What does *legato* mean?' asked Isolde. 'No, it does not mean scratch your left foot.' She gave Anna a brief hug.

Anna had been practising a simplified piano version of a Beethoven song, *The Wonder Rose*.

'Sit with a straight back and bring out those top notes. More strength in the right-hand fourth and fifth fingers.' She pencilled in some fingering.

Christoph sat staring at a page of Latin. Distractedly he imagined Uta's enticing shape which her uniform's thick leather coat had not disguised. Its close-fitting cut and belt had in fact emphasised the isthmus between her chest and pelvis. She was both lithe and alluring.

So why had Bauss asked to see them? An armchair warrior giving them an obvious warning? Corporal Dietl could have done that.

'Good. The *arpeggios* were smoother ... but you missed out four bars.'

'Did I?'

'The examiner might think he's just nodded off, but we can't rely on it.'

Knuckles knocked on their solid if slightly skewed rhomboidal door.

'Next week's scales; B major and B minor.'

Anna's father entered. 'You've replaced the snapped E string?'

'You've a good ear, Herr Esel.'

He handed her three one-Mark notes.

He was the Deputy Mayor of Essbach and since his

name meant 'donkey', he was popularly said to be in receipt of some very juicy carrots.

Isolde wore an off-white cardigan with one original button and two odd ones and a faded blue dress. Skirts or dresses a little below the knee were then *de rigueur* for girls, even if skating or ski-ing.

Could Herr Esel help with solving their father's death? She eyed the hairs which stuck out of his nostrils like pencil leads. But no. Such people were too shrewd to interfere in those affairs.

She managed a smile. 'See you next week, Anna.'

*   *   *   *

The little two-cylinder F9 van stood in the icy-cold air of the transport shed, where it refused to start.

Two energetic rotations of the crank-handle also elicited no encouraging signs.

Corporal Dietl lifted the bonnet, removed the distributor cap and the rotor-arm and scraped and dried both it and its contacts. No success. She fetched a box-spanner from the bench, unscrewed the spark-plugs and cleaned them with some fine emery-cloth. A few drops of petrol and some highly inflammable xylene and methanol carburettor cleaner preceded her replacing the plugs. Stubbornly it still would not ignite, so she summoned Herr Brumm, the duty mechanic.

With half-frozen hands, she went into the main building, washed them slowly in hot water, then headed for the canteen, where as she hung her coat on a peg, a hefty cleaning girl barged past, smiling to herself.

With a bowl of hot broth and a roll, she sat down.

Udo Eckman, also buying lunch, joined her.

'Good afternoon, Captain.'

'Good afternoon, Uta.' He salted his meal. 'Our Chief now has another bee in his bonnet.'

'Oh?'

'He's sending Jörg off on some wild goose chase. Isolde Lyskirchen? Heard of her?'

'Yes. Still, she's only a single bee, not a hive.'

Eckman tackled his two fat sausages, pickled cabbage and potatoes.

'Did you manage to find someone to take to the ballet?'

He arrested his chewing. 'What do you mean, "Did I manage?" You know me better than that.'

'Yes, quite.'

Eckman grinned.

She wondered who? Probably one of the typists whose bottoms he was regularly pinching.

He glanced at the clock. 'My half-day.'

Herr Brumm appeared. 'I've left it ticking over. You'd put the rotor-arm back in upside-down.'

'Thanks.'

Udo grinned. 'No wonder it wouldn't start.' This came scrambled through a mouthful of Sauerkraut.

The old Landgraves would have struck him off the guest list.

*   *   *   *

Azure plaster pillars, gilded acanthus leaves and dancing Muses adorned the proscenium arch, whilst worn red velvet seats completed the fading grandeur of Essbach's provincial theatre.

With quasi-gallantry Udo ushered Greta into the second row of the balcony. 'The best seats in the house.'

A giant Russian sergeant sat next to Greta. She wore a grey skirt and tunic, this last with red collar flashes.

'The next thing is, she'll get stuck in her seat,' Udo whispered.

She turned her jut-jawed face round to glower at them.

A ballet company from Magdeburg performed Adolphe Adam's *Giselle*. The stage was barely broad enough, yet they were so exact and graceful.

Udo wore a crisp white shirt, a neatly knotted tie and a decent enough suit. He sported a red silk bandanna in his jacket's top pocket – a touch spivish – and his hair was slicked sideways from a conventional left-sided parting.

He gazed at Greta's silhouette, its face lit with light from the stage. She pretended simply to watch the dancers, but placed a forearm on the arm-rest between their seats. Another's hand descended gently on top of it.

He stroked it for a time, until she rotated her forearm to be palm upwards. Then their fingers intertwined.

Greta had on a red satin-like blouse with a silver brooch just beneath its neck-line and a maroon pinafore dress. Her hair had a slight natural curl and was silkier and more neatly combed than usual. Her largish breasts were evident and her tan-coloured handbag lay on her lap. She looked warm and attractive and emitted the soft glow of wanting to be ravished.

Udo opened a wooden box. He leant over so that their shoulders touched and with finger and thumb, pushed a cube of Turkish delight into her mouth.

With his lips touching her ear, he whispered, 'A sweet for my sweet.' He pecked her cheek. 'From Bulgaria, via a special Party envoy ... and our own private quartermaster.'

He returned his attention to the ballet. She leant fractionally sideways and allowed her head to tilt so as to rest on his shoulder. The interval curtain descended and they kissed.

Her head swam. This bore promise. Perhaps in a few days she would tell her senescent grandmother how wonderful her new boyfriend was?

In the second act, a mordant blue moonlight shone down on the dancers in the graveyard, whose short diaphanous gauze dresses rose and fell.

The ethereal scenery of blue-tinted greys and deep sage greens added to the pageantry. Nadia Kukolnika in the title role, was so agile.

The Wilis in the drama were wronged female spirits, who deserted in love, danced each cheating man to his death.

Udo, like her, came from a troubled background. Both too, were tough and knew what they wanted. Were they perhaps well-matched?

Udo had read her file. Married then deserted.

As the performance ended, a self-centred craving welled up in her. Outside, in the early evening twilight, Udo invited her to his flat for 'coffee'. She could not restrain a smile.

'My coffee is good ... but you – when stirred – will be delicious.' He squeezed her into a darkened doorway and they exchanged long slobbery and breath-stopping smooches. He pulled her firmly into himself, so that their fronts were pressed together, a contact which further incited their mutual passion.

*   *   *   *

The light underpowered police van hiccoughed its way out of Essbach, through the knot of frosted indigent dwellings at Edstedt and then on into the white rural wilderness of forests and low hills. Snow-drifts in geometrical arcs lay strung between barns and hillocks.

The lane entered an s-bend, which took it up onto a bridge over the railway. Here Uta stopped, climbed out and leant on the parapet, absorbing the stark beauty of the scene.

The railway ahead divided. The main line curved slightly to the left, whilst the branch to Hollern swung away to the right. A signal gantry straddled the tracks and above the dim outline of its steelwork various purple, red and white lights glinted behind the semaphores. With the encroaching gloom, the oil-lamps behind their coloured glasses glowed more strongly; so very kaleidoscopic.

Uta had on an extra jersey and her coat collar and lapels were turned up and buttoned together. Moisture from the freezing damp air glistened as tiny water droplets condensed onto her serge-lined leather coat, forming a sheen on both its creases and smoother parts, as the first fitful rays of a broad sickle moon caught it.

It was bitterly cold.

The road ran parallel to the line to Hollern. Initially a meadow separated them, then both burrowed into a wood. The fir trees stood rigid, under the weight of snow on their boughs.

Her watch read ten to four. In the wood, it became much darker. The van's weak headlight beams splashed the lower trunks of the trees with a fleeting yellow light. She reached a clearing and stopped, switched off the lights and climbed out.

Here tuffets of cowbane and knots of ground elder poked through the thinner blanket of snow. A hedge of hazel and an albescent hawthorn bush were entangled like barbed yet frozen lovers.

A path through the eerie firs, marked by deep snow-trodden dimples, emerged beside the railway line. The bullhead rails, protruding through the snow, gleamed like platinum in the moonlight. To her right lay the dimly-lit signal-box.

As she neared this haven of warmth and light, a figure moved around inside, illumined by an oil-lamp and the glow of a stove.

Five courses of large stone blocks supported the raised custard-coloured wooden cabin.

She climbed the steps to the door and knocked. After a scraping of feet, it opened.

'Hullo,' she said and entered.

A thin fellow in his thirties, wearing blue overalls and a high-necked woolly, closed the door.

'I'm Corporal Dietl of the *Grenzpolizei*.' She smiled tentatively to allay his anxiety.

'Terenz Hüttner, signalman.'

He had been sat beside a little table with an exercise book and a text-book propped up behind it, when a hemispherical bell had pinged three times and he had had to come to his feet, pull two levers forward and then hit a brass knob to send an acknowledging ping back in the Essbach direction.

A lever-frame with blue and red painted cast-iron levers was positioned in front of the windows. On a transom board above these, polished electric bells and dials glinted, connected by neatly laid out red blue and black wiring. A small iron stove, with an enamel coffee-can on it, radiated a most welcome warmth. There were also a row of linked-up batteries, a tin lunch-box, a pile of fire-wood cut in shortish lengths and a rack of tools.

'I believe that Christoph Lyskirchen works here?'

Her pert feminine nymph-like form gave a milder or less threatening effect than would that of a male officer.

'Yes, but he's on nights for three days.'

Her eyes were bright and he noted the slightly concave curve of her nose.

She was silently aware of having an effect upon him. 'What are you studying?' She indicated his books.

'Chemistry and Latin. If I can pass those examinations this summer, I've matriculated in enough subjects to enter technical college.' He seemed guarded though not obsequious, taught by recent history no doubt, to think before he spoke.

Her black coat, gloves, boots, holster, handbag and home-knitted stockings were softened by her pale though shiny face.

The verb 'amplexor' – to embrace – flashed through his mind.

She gave a second limited smile. 'Is Lyskirchen a good colleague?'

Terenz rubbed his chin. 'He's punctual ... efficient ... '

66

'And how do you regard him in other ways?'

'He's a lot on his mind. His father died a few months back and the girl he's seeing is … well, not the kindest I suspect.' He paused. 'I only speak to him at hand-overs.'

The girl's effective way intoxicated him a little and he detected her underlying humanity. 'He studies Latin too … and writes plays.'

'Plays? About what?'

'He's had a children's pantomime accepted at the Rudolf Engelhofer Volksschule … in rhyming verse.'

'Oh?'

'He left the first act here one day … quite witty, but … "No one is born a master," to quote.'

'Inventive though.'

'Written on cut-open cereal packets, to save on paper.'

The box trembled. Two wavering white lights on an engine's buffer-beam approached and the mechanical pounding grew gradually louder. This engine, more sensed than seen as it disgorged clouds of dark smoke and white steam was followed by the vague shapes of goods wagons with the regular beat of their cast-steel wheels on the joints in the track

The din receded, but the smell of coal dust, smoke and warm nebulised oil briefly permeated the box.

Terenz pushed a lever back, depressed a knob on one of the telegraphs at the left-hand end of the box and a needle on its dial swept from the red area over to the blue. He then tapped a knob at the right-hand end of the box three times which rang a bell, which Uta guessed would be repeated in the next box out towards Hollern. An acknowledging ping of the bell came back and the light beside it went out.

'So much smoke,' she remarked.

'A good crew can do a run on half the coal of a poor crew.'

'This is the line to Hollern? Not the main line?'

'Yes, but this box also controls the Rohrdorf sidings over there where long-distance goods trains are marshalled.'

Uta nodded thoughtfully.

'But ... may I ask an extraneous question?'

'Pray proceed with your extraneous question,' she smiled cryptically.

'What's going on in that dilapidated old carriage along there?' He jabbed a thumb to indicate the direction. 'It's on that spur to the abandoned quarry.'

'I've no idea. What makes you think anything's going on?'

'It's a disused sleeper-carriage and a week ago it was shunted there. We were told to keep clear of it.'

'By whom?'

'By our supervisor.'

'I've not heard anything. Do you suspect something odd?' Her fingers touched his cuff and she leant forwards slightly.

'Occasionally cars come and go,' he said simply, 'fairly smart ones ... And once I spotted a man and a woman in quite classy clothes ... '

'I'll wander along and have a look.'

'Is that wise?'

'I don't know.'

Could this carriage be Joos's base of operations ... or his tinned cheese store? Uta was always phlegmatic, but this time, a little nervous too. Yet she felt impelled to go, to find out about her enemy.

Terenz, touched by her brief though intimate contact, watched her descend the steps and pass in front of the signal-box to be swallowed by the all-pervading darkness.

He sensed danger there under the trees and not only from the goblins and sprites of German folk-lore.

*   *   *   *

Niehaus, in plain clothes, strolled down Quintusweg towards the river, buffeted occasionally by gusts of wind funnelled by the warehouses and mills. He looked up at the broken-nosed gargoyles on a boxed-in baroque church, a decidedly unattractive building of blackened stone. He pushed at the creaky needle-door, set into the larger arched door and entered a gloomy oaken-panelled porch.

Inside, a rack of burnt-out votary candles stood in a corner, with one solitary wick still smouldering. A shaft of light from a high-up window threw a few feeble rays down from its blue and lilac panes of leaded glass. Cherubs beneath the corbels at the tops of the slender pillars, with alabaster faces, pink robes and gold curlicued wings failed to fill the nave with celestial radiance.

He advanced quietly along the aisle. At the farther end of the church, a red sanctuary light glimmered above the altar and two hidden lights were aglow somewhere behind the organ from where odd squeaks emanated. He stopped short of the rood screen and looked at an angel of painted wood. She had an endearing pastoral aura about her rosy cheeks and seemed to look back at Niehaus. A nearby Saint Jerome with a face wrinkled as if marinated in prune juice, seemed less epicurean.

Isolde imagined herself alone in the church. She knelt on a moth-eaten flattened hassock on the passage-boards between ranks of pipes, engaged in tuning the set of flue pipes which belonged to the high-pitched *Blockflöte*. She would adjust one up or down a whisker and then depress a valve. She had some tuning forks and her sense of perfect pitch to assist her.

Niehaus sat in a pew catching partial glimpses of her as she moved about. After she had finished tuning this one rank and had returned to the console to play the scale of F major slowly on it, she returned to the gallery above the slightly raised organ loft. Through a fretwork of carved oak he saw her kneeling on some old boards and with pliers and a screwdriver setting about replacing a broken tracker rod with a new one which her brother had made. A linen thread binding had held the old one temporarily together. She extracted the split-pin which joined it to its backfall.

Clearly she was up to nothing devious so Niehaus stood up and went into the chancel, deliberately making a noise on the flags with his shoes so that she should hear him. He called up to her, 'Good afternoon to you.'

Surprised, she returned his greeting. 'Good afternoon.'

'Are you Fräulein Lyskirchen?'

'Yes.'

Isolde thought that he might be a policeman, so when he said, 'Before you ask, I'm a policeman,' she felt quite relieved.

'What are you doing here?'

'Watching you.'

'Why?'

'I don't know – just obeying orders.' He liked something

about her presence, even though at this stage he had not seen much of her. 'May I come up and join you?'

'If you wish.'

He ascended the nine steps into the so-called 'loft' and she backed out of the cramped area above it and came down. He looked at this remarkably fair if reclusive lass.

'You are the organist here?'

She shrugged briefly as if it were no great achievement.

'Do you receive an honorarium?'

'Fourteen Marks and a two kilos of candle stubs a month.'

There was a light over the pedals and another over the two manuals, the ledge which held the music and the row of stops on each side. She sat herself on the long straight fixed stool and looked sideways at where he stood.

'Where are you from?' he asked.

'Munich originally, but my parents moved around a lot.'

He nodded. 'The upheavals of the war? Living with people who are not your own kith and kin?'

'True, but I don't feel isolated. I have a brother and there's companionship at the University and here. My mother though is now in Pütnitz, so I miss her.'

She felt safer in the church than in her flat and however run-down and even tawdry it might appear to the casual passer-by – the statue of the Virgin and Child, the stations of the Cross and the other Catholic paraphernalia – to her everything in it hinted at an inestimable wonder.

She wore a cobalt blue dress with a tie-behind belt of the same colour, a cream lace collar and narrow sleeves with small buttoned cuffs. On top of this she had a thickish sloppy woolly of her brother's to fight the chill in this dowdy cavernous place. Her face however appeared to Niehaus, bright and engaging.

'I have never really liked organ music ... too thunderous.'

'Some organists do overdo the volume, true ... but it can be simple.'

'Will you play something?'

She looked at him with quiet curiosity, before taking up a piece of music from a shelf behind her. She pulled out a couple of stops and said, 'This is from Bach's "Coffee Cantata".'

'Not his "Chocolate with Two Scoops of Ice-cream Cantata"?'

'No,' she said with a smile.

*   *   *   *

A wind had sprung up and gusts blew snow off the trees as Uta advanced beside the railway line. The settled snow looked grey beneath the canopy of branches, in the dark underbelly of the pine-wood. She had a police torch in her handbag, but dared not use it. Some of the wind-dislodged flakes melted on her face or crept down the inside of her collar.

An abandoned vineyard, a ruined tower and a rocky gorge, where evil hobgoblins were said to dwell, lay just to the north.

She passed a signal post and a curiously shaped boulder, then the wood fell back, giving way to wispy bushes of whin or blackthorn, with their thorny stems and serrated leaves.

Her boots crunched the powdery and undinted snow.

The hidden twigs were wet, but some snapped if trodden on.

A frame of rusty crude iron-work became suddenly visible. A massive baulk of splintered timber lay bolted horizontally to it, which she now saw formed a buffer-stop. Beyond it, she made out the silhouette of the carriage almost end-on in this drear snow-clad panorama.

She stopped beside a prickly juniper bush to listen and watch. There were no sounds and no lights as far as she could tell, so she approached the eight-wheeled monster, treading warily beside its grim iron bogies and axle-boxes. Its main chassis girders were above the height of her head, but at each end were vertical running steps which led up to a wrought-iron-balustraded balcony.

After circumnavigating the carriage, she climbed one of these sets of steps onto a balcony. On the door which led into the main body of the carriage the red and grey paint of East German nationalisation was flaking off to reveal the blue and cream livery of its pre-war owners.

She turned the handle and shoved the door with her shoulder. It opened. In the deep shadows, she could make out a long saloon-like compartment with upholstered seats facing inwards and a few cardboard boxes stacked on them. Her heart beat quickly. Although seemingly quite alone, she still dared not risk using her torch. Prising open a box, shiny tins without labels greeted her, the same she thought, as those on Thilo's sledge. She strained her eyes, peering round for more precise clues. Like a diver in a sunken ship, she groped her way into the corridor and in the first sleeping compartment found – more by touch than sight – a wad of thickish paper. She took it back to the saloon and made it out to be a folded linen-backed map and an envelope labelled 'Die Deutsche Notenbank der DDR'.

She slid it into her handbag and had just started to delve deeper for a blue wax crayon with which to place a mark on each of the cartons, when the roar of a car engine bursting through the nearby trees made her jump. Two powerful head-lamps lurched and oscillated down a forestry track towards her.

She fled the interior, closing the door, half-hotched and half-jumped off the balcony and threw herself down in a clump of withered brittle stems which snapped briskly under her weight.

The car's beams swung round and Uta on the other side of the carriage – looking across the rusty rails beneath it – could make out the old excavated quarry's enclave. It had steep sides with snow-decked baby firs bordering its top edges and the brown oxidized hulks of some old stone-crushing machinery.

The car slewed to a halt and the engine died but its side-lights stayed on, casting a weak sector of light towards the carriage. Two figures emerged. The Corporal discerned Joos's tall shape in its smart coat in front of the car's lights and then a slim elegant woman with a fur hat.

'So it ended in a shoot-out; "Freya" versus the *Bundespolizei*.'

Joos's merciless, knife-like tones cut the air. 'Well if she's dead, then she can't talk.'

'No. She's only ... '

The grinding and straining of an approaching engine drowned out their subsequent dialogue.

Walking stiffly in the direction of the railway carriage, the woman halted abruptly. Uta lying motionlessly saw her point to the fresh imprints in the snow. Like sniffer dogs they started to follow them.

The shunting engine drew close. Ripples of bumps moved back and forth along its string of loose-coupled trucks. Uta had thought to tight-rope walk along a rail as escapees walk in streams to lose their scent and shake off trackers, but that was now not possible.

As the crescendo of whooshing peaked and clouds of opaque steam hissed from the engine's cylinders so obscuring her, the Corporal retreated thirty paces before kneeling down again in a thicket of wilting undergrowth. The engine's din faded, but her pursuers had found a torch and its light started to slice the night-darkened foliage in wide arcs. Uta lay flat and with her head down so far as was consistent with using her eyeballs at maximum elevation to observe the enemy. A mosaic of stalk-filtered light passed ineffectually over her.

The Minister's niece chose to search the opposite end of the clearing to where the intruder lay.

As she took this chance to withdraw further, Uta's right ankle twisted over in a hidden rut. In trying to use her other foot to stabilise herself, it caught in an invisible tangle of brambles, spun her round and she fell into a faggot of frozen briers and nettles.

The woman – who presumably equated to the sobriquet *Goneril* on Bauss's list – heard the crackling of bracken and strode unerringly towards the prone form. The Corporal's dark clothing did not help on the white ground. Her nose was a hair's breadth from the snow and her arms were crooked forward in front of her.

The hostile beam probed a bush, wavered on a patch of gravel, then settled immovably on her flattened cat-like form. It jabbed at her eyes as she lay pressed into the snow and a cluster of weeds.

The huntress called out sharply, 'Edgar, I've found him.' Her high-pitched voice scythed the air.

Joos with his pistol drawn approached. The game was up. Uta rose tremblingly to her feet. Small clumps of snow clung to parts of her clothing. The torch beam rose with her.

Joos skidded on a snow-covered frozen puddle, stumbled on a branch and fell inelegantly into some sparse though longish vegetation. He swore and struggled to his feet.

Uta stood mutely. The presence of Luise Stege should inhibit Joos from anything too savage.

'Well well, if it isn't the indefatigable Corporal Dietl again. Why are you spying on us?'

She winced, for the glare of the torch dazzled her and spoke with a shaky voice. 'Herr Joos, I was visiting the signal-box on police business … and the signalman … '

' … told you that something fishy was going on?' A gleam of delight lurked in his malignant features.

She lowered her head. 'He asked what was happening here.'

'So you came to investigate?'

'It is only coincidence that we have met twice.' There was something of protestation in her voice, an assertion that she was being truthful.

'You are *too* efficient,' he stated. His recollection of her previous intransigence sparked an urge for revenge.

Bizarrely, she wondered if he had ever been loved.

He spoke to his companion. 'This policewoman has interfered with us before, Luise.' His intention was to arrange a scene for just the two of them. 'Leave this to me. Go inside the carriage.' She shrugged and did as he asked.

Joos strode forward a pace and grabbed Uta by her coat lapels which were again buttoned together in front of her throat. Whilst clutching these in his left hand he growled softly, 'Now, we are going to have an entertaining "exchange".' He permitted himself a faint smile as he flicked its safety catch back on and repocketed his weapon.

She reiterated her solemn affirmation that she was there by mere chance.

His accomplice, who now stood Juliet-like on the carriage's end balcony, called with a trace of warning in her tone. 'Edgar, what are you going to do?'

'Go inside,' he rasped. 'This is my field.' She did so, closing the door behind her.

They were alone in the near darkness. As he turned back, Uta saw the vulture-like swerve of his bowed nose. His face flamed dully yet irascibly like a red warning beacon. With Luise gone, he abandoned his suave pose and shook her fiercely. 'Do you think I'm stupid? Who's behind this?'

She tried to bow her head but it was too strait-jacketed by his fist's tight grasp of her lapels. 'Not stupid Herr Joos, but desperate perhaps.' She did not know why she had said that.

He eyed her form in a way she did not like. It was not merely unwelcome curiosity, but a desire to ravish or harm her.

In a paroxysm he jerked her towards himself. 'Don't look condescendingly at me.'

By a glimmer of moonlight which found breaks in the ribbon-like clouds, he espied her neatly pointed breasts again for as she breathed the two white reflective spots on their curved surfaces rose and fell.

He would bundle her into the trees and rape her ... on some nice comfy fir twigs. 'Comfy for her,' he thought. He would be comfy anyway, since he would be on top of her. His free right hand came up to probe her lower feminine parts.

'No you don't.' Her hands seized his right hand.

They were inarbitrarily locked together.

Joos felt trapped by his passions, because their world had become egalitarian but not permissive, at least not so far as girls like Uta and towns like Essbach were concerned.

His toe-caps gleamed. The tips of their noses, the tips of her breasts and their gloved knuckles all shone as white dots, expressively sinister in their contrast to the surrounding blackness.

'I enjoy exercising my male rights over pretty girls ... especially defiant ones.' He thought to lull her into a static numbness. 'It does them good to have an occasional jumping-cracker in their knickers ... ' Expecting to catch her unawares, he tried suddenly to hurl her to the ground, but she braced herself in the nick of time. He kicked her left shin, intending to throw her sideways as her leg gave way, but again she stood firm. Being mentally limp, she hardly felt pain. His own ineffectiveness annoyed him.

Her police-issue boots had good thick rubber grips.

The hard-edged quarter-moon nudged the tops of the

screen of sharp-pointed black firs. In this masculine world of war and iron, feminine input and enchantment were a rarity. Uta was the sparkle he needed to enliven his day's dismal grey porridge. The Dorian gods of pillage and devastation wished to abuse her, to deny her the status of the Ionian goddesses of dancing and wine and love.

He wanted to make her cower and submit, but there was still the constraint of Luise ... unless he dragged her some distance away. His thoughts equated copulating with power.

One handicap in overcoming her lay with his slippery leather-soled shoes. He had mislaid the broad heavy stud-bearing rubber bands which could be pulled on over them. She seemed stronger too tonight than in Ursulinenklosterweg.

He snatched his right hand free and lunged it at her to squeeze her left breast and drive her backwards, but this too was parried and again he was repulsed. She was not quick enough though to dodge the forceful punch which followed. She stumbled backwards and fell into some shrivelled thistles. This lying, half-reclining posture seemed the ultimate cue.

Her pistol was a Walther P38. These were standard *Wehrmacht* issue from 1937 until the end of the war. She was quite a good shot, at least on the ranges. A trace of moonlight caught her silvery face and he saw faintly on it a dark area of blood. She edged her right hand down towards her holster, but he smoothly extracted his pistol first and smiled. 'Keep your hands away from your belt. Get up and turn around. When I've disarmed you, walk along that track over there.'

She hesitated for five or six seconds.

'Move!' He swung his right leg to give her a hefty kick in the thigh, but without warning his left foot slithered on another snow-hidden frozen puddle. Like a snatched marionette his body lurched and overbalanced. He screwed round on his knee and his weapon flew up into the air to land with an unlocatable flop some distance away. He reflexly grabbed the stump of a dead sapling, which wrenched his shoulder violently. As he struggled to his feet, an excruciating pain seized him. Sinking onto his knees, a huge curved thorn tore his coat. His right shoulder had been dislocated. His plan to pin Uta to the wet mossy forest floor and molest her soft body with luxurious force had been foiled.

Uta raised herself up onto her elbows and slid backwards in the snow.

Using three limbs he gingerly rose and adopted the stooped gait of a gorilla. A good genie had acted on her behalf. With his eyes smouldering, Joos slunk slowly off to lick his wounds.

She touched her face with her right hand. Her glove spread the still oozing blood from her lip and nostrils. The blow had hit her nose and cut the left side of her upper lip. She took out a handkerchief and put it to her wounds.

She stood up on jelly-like legs and leant back against a young spruce. On discovering that she had no immediate fears, she decided to return via the signal-box and the police van to town.

Bending over to recover her hat, a sheaf of paper oblongs caught her eye; a wad of banknotes held in a clip. Opening its flap, she popped it into her handbag which she then hung from her shoulder before retracing her steps to the signal cabin.

*   *   *   *

Isolde was not a virtuoso organist, but played in a style which whilst firm and clear, was quite light and detached. *Fair Flowers* ended.

'This organ's in poor repair. Luckily the blower motor keeps going, though it dates from 1922.'

Niehaus agreed that these were lean times.

It seemed like the right time to exit, but the policeman felt drawn both by Isolde and this abstract world of music. His eyes flitted over the rows of stops with their names etched into their black knobs – *Prinzipal, Geigen, Subbass, Waldflöte* – she watched him and pointed to the last of these. 'That's the best stop on this organ.'

As he seemed reluctant to leave, she asked, 'Could I impose on you? Would you help me glue down two warped planks on the wind chest? It's leaking air through the cracks and the screws are too tight for me to loosen.'

'Happily ... and afterwards could I play a few notes?'

'We must do that first, because of leaving the glue to dry.'

He removed his light grey mackintosh.

'Would you like to play a hymn?' She picked up a battered hymnal.

He came round to her right side and sat beside her on the long broad polished oak plank which formed the organ stool. There, in the island of light cast by the bulb fixed above the music ledge, he looked at the rather stained keys. 'Could we try *Lasst uns erfreuen?*'

She pulled out the *Hohlflöte* stop and played a few bars on the upper keyboard.

'Could I just play the top line?'

She found the right page, propped it up and stopped the pages from turning by anchoring them with clothes-pegs.

'You have a go whilst I light the gas ring under the fish glue in the vestry.'

She left him for a minute or two and he played the melody line. He looked around at the lovely painted wooden angel who stood on bunches of dusty grapes. Her cherry-tinged cheeks smiled down at him. Isolde came back. 'Curl your fingers more.'

'Yes. I remember that. My mother told me to imagine I was holding an orange.'

'I haven't seen an orange for ... fifteen years.' She pulled out a second stop inscribed *Dulzian*. 'If we combine a reed and a flue stop of the same pitch, we get this.' She made a sign for him to play the first line again and he could hear that it was a pleasing mix.

'Don't release the notes too early.'

Finally he played the soprano line on the choir manual using the distinctively toned oboe stop and she played the other voices using quieter stops on the great organ and the pedal-board. She pulled her sleeves slightly back and her feet in black canvas slippers, dabbed daintily at the large wooden bars, which as it was an old organ were parallel and not set as a fan.

He set about unscrewing the corroded woodscrews which held the two bowed and ill-fitting oak planks in place. He sweated and puffed but some new strength helped him to undo them. They applied the boiling glue to their edges, put them back and he screwed them down firmly. Lastly they dribbled some of the bubbling treacly glue into a few small crevices to further improve the seal.

She inclined her head and thanked him. He withdrew a rare bar of dark chocolate from an inside coat pocket. 'Nine days early, but wishing you a peaceful Christmas.'

On leaving the church, forbidding brick buildings, iron bridges and rough flagstones greeted him in the dark empty sleet-whipped street. Such were the towns here, whilst the countryside bore the burdens of heavy agricultural quotas.

Niehaus stood there, his hands in his coat pockets, studying this patch of existence in which he found himself.

The red rays from an unseen furnace caught some nearby roof ridges and made them glow like the embers of a dying fire. The street was deeply silent.

Then a factory siren signalled five o'clock and a trickle of shabbily clad men and girls left their shift at Bebel's copper foundry.

A Latin saw came to him. 'Know you not by how little wisdom the world is governed?'

*   *   *   *

The icy wind which had sprung up now drove the disturbed snow into Corporal Dietl's back as she stumbled back towards the signal-box.

The signal post which stood alongside the odd-shaped rock was composed of riveted plates and angle-girders – and so without interstices – thus differing from the commoner lattice-girder masts. For a minute or two she clung to it, exhausted and trembling.

Terenz had sallied out with a large blow-lamp to thaw some of the pulley and crank bearings so that the wires and rods to the signals and points should not seize up. Then with a spade, he scraped snow out from between the blades of the points.

Next he ran into the battered and distraught policewoman and saw the congealed blood on her nose and lip.

He preferred to engage with girls at a distance, but here was clear evidence of a fracas and a need for help. Blood from her bruised nose was already tracking up around her left eye, so preparing to blacken it.

He steered her up the signal-box steps and sat her down beside the stove. He shed his thick jacket and knelt to inspect her face. 'Only a small cut to the upper lip. I shouldn't think it needs a stitch. Head wounds often bleed a lot and so seem worse than they are. Is this the first time your loveliness has been blighted?'

She managed a half-smile.

'Did you trip over?'

'No. I was punched.'

Terenz was speechless for a moment.

Her nostrils were full of encrusted blood and her nose displayed a swollen bridge.

'If they can assault you, they really are dangerous.'

'They are very high-ranking. Untouchable.'

He poured some coffee from the can on the stove and gave her one of the cheese rolls from his lunch-box, which she accepted without demur. Standing, she unbuckled her belt and took off her coat, opened the door and shook the snow off it. She sat down again in her blue woolly and skirt and felt the bruise on her shin from Joos's kick.

Terenz warmed some water and with a piece of clean rag, soaked and dissolved some of the matted blood. 'We used to have some salt and dried rosemary here in a jar, but it's gone, but the cut doesn't look dirty.'

She started to recover as the hot coffee and the bread spread their influence. She peered into her handbag at the newly acquired money and was able to remove six used ten-Mark notes without exposing their larger denomination cousins. 'Take these.'

'No no. I don't need payment.'

'Please?'

He looked unsure. 'Why?'

'It's from those villains ... but they don't know.'

He hesitated, then took the notes. 'I'll use them on more course books. Thanks.'

She rolled her one fully open eye.

He poured himself coffee too and sat on the rack of accumulators. 'I did my apprenticeship at the locomotive works in Weimar. In its heyday it had been a first-class engineering set-up ... but now few there have any real mechanical aptitude. If the engines break down so what?'

She smiled. 'Forgive me if I don't feel like talking.'

'Quite all right. In the old days, Saturday mornings were for grinding and sharpening tools and for overhauling the machinery, but now in an ill-judged drive to increase output, they're also given over to shoddy production.'

Uta was grateful for the warmth, the food and the human contact.

She half-dreamt of the citadel of darkness. His long

shadow spun round, its dark eyes narrowing, his lips thin … and the magical evil of his art; a terrible wood-louse covered in black syrup.

She was asleep.

A golden comb of light edged the tops of the black trees and below the meadows were a dark grey. He dragged her along until …

Terenz shook her gently. 'We might soon be snowed in. It's falling heavily again.'

'Oh … yes.'

She roused herself and started to put on her outdoor attire.

'If those thugs come, say I came to inquire about Lyskirchen.'

'Will they believe it?'

'Well it's the truth.'

She left and waded back to the van which luckily was parked in the epicentre of an eddy where little snow had fallen.

Six sheep at a gate munched at a bale of fodder in the half-blizzard. She climbed onto the gate to pat one, but they all scampered back a few yards, then stood and watched her, silent and dumb.

The F9's engine started. She let it tick over for a few minutes to warm up whilst brushing snow off the windows. With a muffled drubbing of its snow-chains on the thick rug of snow it rumbled back to the outskirts of Essbach.

Here Uta stopped and laid out the small bundle of notes on the ribbed leather seat beside her. Using her torch she counted four fifty-Mark notes – the highest denomination then circulating in East German currency or Ostmarks – eight West German notes and twenty American ten-dollar bills.

Banknotes seemed to fit with this clique's being racketeers. The possession of foreign notes was supposedly illegal.

There was a small tear in the lining of her police handbag and by slightly extending this rent, she was able to slide the flattened-out notes behind its fabric. As to the map it was of the area around the Rohrdorf quarry, rather simple and quite old. Rings had been drawn on bits of it and roughly cross-hatched with a crimson crayon.

*   *   *   *

In his office, Bauss ate an in-house apple-puff with his coffee. The cakes here were very good, indeed someone had suggested that this was why this sub-division was regarded as a first-class unit.

No hurry to go home. His flat held little appeal unless Carine were there.

Isolde, like an angel come down from heaven, scared him. Untainted by passion and if angry too wise to nurture it, she would shed tears only if alone. Hers was a purity neither affected nor advertised.

He sensed his persona to be under a reciprocal siege.

'Sussi, I love you.' At times he could not utter this, so deep were the scars.

The duty sergeant knocked.

'Still working, Sir?' He handed the Chief a large sealed envelope. 'From Corporal Dietl.'

He opened it and looked at the stolen map and the historic bank documents copied by 'Freya'. A note said they had come from the old railway carriage, where Joos seemed to operate from.

'What the blazes is she up to?' He looked up. 'Er …
thank you, Sergeant.'

Was he 'nemo' – nobody? With Susanne he would be
Lorenz, but without her he was no one.

The gentle flame of true love makes us human, whilst
rejection spurs a craving for war, a scent not calmed by the
kisses of a skittish maid … even his sweet Carine.

CHAPTER FIVE

Greta and Udo tumbled through the front-door of his flat. He switched on the kitchen light, set about making coffee and sliced up a Paradise cake, an oblong block with cherries and almonds on top.

'I enjoyed the ballet.'

A cauldron of unanalysed emotions bubbled within her. Partly she envied the agility of the dancers at the matinée, but also there lurked in the wings, the boredom of one who no longer cares.

Udo hummed a tune whilst pouring the coffee.

She gulped some down, then Udo escorted her into the dark pit of his bedroom.

They had both rejected gold coinage for one of debased or lead-alloyed silver.

Yet perhaps this impure concoction of old tar and brick-dust could be baked into a beautiful vase?

Udo spun her round and rolled her swiftly back onto the bed, one hand clutching a largish breast, a common though succulent fruit.

He navigated the familiar waterways and Greta allowed the rapid or even improper pace of his advances.

She hated his bristly moustache when he kissed her. Its prickles irritated her.

Her hand cajoled his sodden sticky nub to assimilate itself into her proffered orifice and so began a succession of horizontal gymnastics.

The sun had shone in Munich and Lorenz had expected to see Susanne Dettmann leaving the infirmary that day in February 1930. The bright beacon of his heart must have left by another exit because later her friend said that she had been on the early shift. Had she deliberately avoided his ambush? He had planned to ask her to the cinema and to hold her hand.

In the long main corridor, with its light grey and pale yellow tiling, he had sat on a hard oak seat, gazing at the prim erect nurses and the bent old porters walking purposefully back and forth.

'Sussi, I love you so deeply,' he wept inwardly, for that was the greatest balm to his poor soul.

In her neat navy mack and wide-brimmed felt hat, he would approach her with fresh hope in his heart only to receive a sharp, 'No!' or a dismissive, 'We can't arrange it like this.'

His flat-mates had said that if he suggested any further stratagems to woo her, they would tie him to his bed and beat his head with a bottle until he saw sense.

Yet he could not rid himself of his unique feelings towards her. That year – 1929 – affected his whole life, for he reflected on her rebuffs for the rest of his days.

A brisk series of raps on his door arrested these recurrent meanderings. 'Er … come in.'

Niehaus appeared in a white shirt with a sand-coloured tie and dark grey flannels.

'Well?'

'I've done as you asked, Herr Oberkommissar,' said Jörg brightly.

'You tracked her?'

'A piece of cake, Sir. I've spent half the afternoon sat beside her, learning about and helping to repair the organ at the Johanneskirche.'

The desk lamp's green shade threw a conical beam across the blotter and illumined Bauss's plump fingers.

'So, you sat beside her? Is she likely to do anything then? Surveillance is supposed to be covert.'

'I am sure Sir, that she is up to nothing. It's just not in her nature.'

'So, she enchanted you … with music?'

'In the war Sir, some freezing German soldiers heard some Russian musicians playing and called out, "Play Bach for us," and astonishingly the foe obliged.'

'I think that was at Stalingrad?'

The Chief showed a newspaper to Jörg and indicated an article. '*Der Rotes Krokodil* missile. Isolde's father once worked on it.'

Niehaus surveyed it briefly. 'Americans refer to rockets as "ballistic" missiles. If they have engines and variable fins then they are non-ballistic.'

'True. "$\beta\alpha\lambda\lambda\omega$" is "to throw". Perhaps just to sound impressive?

Anyway, thank you Jörg.'

The lieutenant left.

He had even visited the high school Susanne had attended in Innsbruck.

He had established – belatedly – that at the war's end Ekkehard and Christoph had dwelt near Essbach. Then after a few months Isolde had joined them. Susanne though had lingered in the West for over a year. 'Evading your sham husband?'

After the engineered death of that desiccated cod, Lorenz had 'bumped into' Susanne, who had said huskily, 'I should have guessed.'

With stolid zeal, he had asked, 'Don't judge me. Can we not just melt into one another … as it always should have been?'

She had walked shakily away and then exiled herself to Ribnitz on the Baltic coast, to sew flags for inshore patrol boats.

And now her daughter seemed intent on causing him to implode. Isolde's going from A to B by a straight line with an aura of impassive simplicity belied some hidden warrior-like intuition.

This wraith-like emissary, this offspring, this dissembler, had become the new epicentre of his being. Sin is far more colourful, more engaging than lifeless virtue, even if doomed.

He would take a trip himself to see what this arch-enchantress was up to.

*   *   *   *

Willibald von Schaar – an amiable former aristocrat – spoke with his sister on the telephone. He mentioned a cheese roll he had to eat for his supper. If he melted such cheese in the oven, it would taste like Camembert.

The eavesdropper stifled a yawn.

He had once lived in Italy and studied the old Tuscan dialect, but was now a school caretaker. He mopped the corridors carefully, swept snow off the steps, strewed salt on them and gazed benignly at the pictures drawn by the infants which were pinned up on the classroom walls. Deep in his heart he wished these lively little tots well.

Did he keep warm enough? Oh yes. His garden lay at the bottom of a railway embankment and about ten tons of coal had appeared back in October when the side of a wagon of a passing coal train had fallen open. He was just wishing her a happy and religious Christmas, when she faded abruptly. Being on a rural line and hence far from the exchange, she was not on a central battery signal as direct current attenuates over longer distances, but was dependent on her own telephone's battery which evidently needed recharging.

Brunhilde Axt next listened in to a Herr Huth – a local politician – and an anonymous trader. These chameleons were too astute to commit telephonic blunders. 'Come to my office on Tuesday.'

Had Brunhilde been out to catch those guilty of illegal misdoings, she would have netted only small fry. In fact she was sifting for clues about this mysterious Rohrdorf quarry, to see if their stirring the pond had caused any frogs to croak?

She wore a mauve suede skirt and a lilac mohair cardigan, both with Parisian outfitters' tags inside. These were outrageously chic for Essbach as was her purple goat-skin handbag.

She sat in Essbach's telephone exchange with a pair of ear-phones over her drawn-back blonde hair and a note-book in which to scribble anything important.

The spacious utilitarian room was high-ceilinged, well-lit and had long frosted windows. The racks holding the long-distance selectors were made from galvanised channel girders. These and the bundles of wires in varied colours had a temporary appearance, reflecting the exchange's constant modifications. A substantial electric heater kept all the apparatus dry.

Ulla, the local girl, doing a regular night-duty shift, disliked such company.

The rule of thumb was to be wary of such 'invaders', but she ventured an odd remark.

They sat on metal swivel-chairs in front of arrays of sockets and small lights. Numbers down the edges and along the top constituted a grid by which each socket's number could be determined.

Their ear-phones had microphones attached and two wires which were plugged into the board.

As Ulla pushed back a lock of hair, a tiny bulb beside socket number 505 lit up. When a caller lifted his ear-piece, it completed a circuit with the exchange and this both rang a buzzer and lit a bulb. She took a rubber-bodied jack-plug with its brass tip and copper ring which was on the end of a red braided flex and pushed it home into 505's socket before depressing a large button with 'SPRICH' on it. 'Number please?' The caller wanted 112. 'Connecting you.' She released the 'SPRICH' button whilst inserting the second plug of the linked pair into 112's socket. A second button initiated a ringing tone on 112's instrument. When answered, 505's light went out and Ulla listened to the first few words to confirm the connection.

Brunhilde retreated for a break, reclining in the manager's armchair and pouring herself a coffee from her vacuum flask.

The lights at 505 and 112 came on, meaning that the call had ended and Ulla pulled out the plugs.

Of the day's calls, one had some potential. A call to the University, to a Dozent Herr Doktor Goitschel about a vacancy.

Sophie Höh named a meeting many summers before, beside a lake and near a wooden white-painted villa. The wooden piles and planking of the jetty had been mirrored in the still water and a curlew's caw had spread eerily over the quiet scene. They had spent the night in a boat-house ... a clear dawn, the gold-edged silhouettes of trees, breakfast on newly-scythed grass ...

Brunhilde envied this long-gone romance; bronze-flecked rings in the stream, a breathlessly still summer morning, a slept-with paramour ...

But more prosaically, this spot sounded like an Abwehr wartime spy school she had heard of. They were linguists, so had they been spies?

Her accomplice, Luise Stege, came in to do a stint.

'One faint possibility ... though we're looking for a needle in a haystack.'

'We haven't found the haystack yet.'

Luise was tall with a hint of self-conscious elegance, a thin straight-edged nose and a prominent mole on her cheek. Her face was elliptical and like her body, slender.

She handed Brunhilde a roll. 'They only had crab paste left.'

'Oh well, caviar at the end of the tunnel ... if we ever find it?'

'Said tunnel has just sprung a leak.'

Axt looked up quizzically.

'I've just come from the hospital. Edgar decided to have a scrap with a police lass and lost.'

'Oh? And he's injured?'

'She dislocated his shoulder.'

Brunhilde smiled faintly. 'That's pretty impressive.'

'My God was he in pain?'

Brunhilde's grin broadened a shade.

'Why the hell did your father and my uncle select him to lead this bloody crazy search?'

They ate their buns and drank coffee and felt better.

Mercury rectifiers flickered, whilst thick copper bus-bars and clicking relays gave the place a modern technological air.

Both had had practical experience with electronics.

The H.V.A. had sent Luise to Africa on a plane with false GB markings, to steal a BOAC Delta radio with a frequency of twelve hundred megacycles per second and then to listen in on stuff about the Mau Mau Uprising.

Brunhilde had been in the Kriegsmarine operations room, near Narvik. 'We were on the *Grille*, which had been Hitler's state yacht. It was camouflage painted in slate grey, pale yellow and dark green. In the conference room there were map-tables with small coloured aircraft and warship models on them ... and question-mark shapes to represent positions given by uncertain sightings or intercepts.'

Brunhilde mentioned Goitschel's call and tore out the page from her note-book. 'His address from the directory is; 2F, Keplerstrasse. Will you go or shall I?'

Luise fancied the walk.

Axt had earlier untangled some wires – blue, orange and black – and tied and labelled them according to which rank of amplifying valves they served.

Was she neurotic, she wondered? She had no lover or husband and was now thirty-six.

Ulla was chatting to a lineman who had come to collect some insulators from the stores. He introduced himself boldly to Brunhilde. 'Wilhelm Hoffman. My first job was here … on the switchboard.'

'You circulate around different posts?'

'Well, I hope it's a slightly upward spiral.'

Her blonde hair had been styled into a stubby coiffure, but more complex than the simple plaits or buns seen in Essbach.

She smiled.

He winked and said, 'Good night.'

*   *   *   *

Bauss changed into his everyday grey trousers, a white shirt with a separate collar and stud, a tie and a knitted waistcoat.

An old police cape hung on a peg. Would it make him look devilish, even boar-like though he lacked the tusks? He chose the standard incognito overcoat and Trilby.

In town, he parked in a small square just as the medieval clock-tower tolled six. Its deep booming tones echoed softly.

The sparse light of the street-lamps glinted on the trampled snow, whilst the icy tracks carved in it by tyres appeared greyish.

The medieval shops and houses were built of gnarled beams filled in with brick. The eighteenth-century ones were of weather-worn stonework, often with contrastingly coloured quoins.

In Syrakusallee a north wind groped its way between the overhanging shops with their steeply-pitched roofs, gable windows and ornate iron-work signs which hung out at right angles.

The Police Chief walked through the archway under the squat clock-tower. Its clock-face had gilded hands and numbers. Its broken medieval guild figures had once danced a short allemande on the hour. On the opposite side of the cobbled Luisenhof, lay Keplerstrasse.

He tilted his hat forward, crossed the square and walked past the stone tenement building where Isolde and her brother lived. It had a wide arched doorway with a curvilinear though well-weathered escutcheon of the old Landgraves of Thuringia above it and an enamelled number '2' beside it, whilst its three floors of identical windows were all flanked by pairs of shutters painted with grey and maroon chevrons. He had often walked furtively past it when Susanne had dwelt there.

A horse and cart clopped by. He glimpsed the pointed studs on the under-side of its horse-shoes to prevent it from slipping.

A tall well-dressed lass was about to enter number two.

'Excuse me? Police.' He produced his warrant. 'May I ask your business here?'

Without speaking, she pulled out her *Staatspolizei* identity card, eyed him coolly and disappeared into the building.

'God,' he muttered. That was *Goneril*. What the hell was she doing here?

He crossed to *Der Alte Essbacher*, a café which

overlooked both the square and the front entrance to the Lyskirchen's flat.

It was above an ironmonger's. A flight of steps, led up to its ornamented doorway. Inside, fake potted palms, framed posters of Marlene Dietrich and other pre-war film stars and an ancient mahogany counter – behind which were brass coffee-bean-grinders, bottle-racks and a collection of old municipal pennons and flags – gave it a dated atmosphere. Two long windows overlooked the square.

The proprietor, Herr Langenbeck, spat out a quid of chewing tobacco and flung a split log into the stove before slamming its iron grating shut. 'Especially for you, Herr Bauss.'

'I feel honoured.' He offered a sardonic smile.

'No dog today?'

'Nero? He's getting old … like all of us.'

Bauss sat at a table beside a window. To his right three card players were absorbed in their game.

A slender serving girl in a black satin dress and a white mini-pinafore came over.

'Good evening, Sabine. You look quite good in the candlelight.'

'And you look quite good in the shadows, Herr Bauss.'

He laughed lightly. 'The *Lappsuppe* ... and an apple juice.' He sneezed.

'Bless you.'

'Usually no one says that, so I have to bless myself.'

'Ah, the penalties of high rank?'

Conrad Lanze, a steam-roller driver who sat nearby in over-mended breeches and a ragged woolly, said, 'When the telegram boy cycled by in the war, we said a prayer for whichever poor devil had died, but we never said one for the nobs.'

He rose and went to catapult ball-bearings around the bagatelle table.

The card players took a break, Sabine took away some used crockery and the Police Chief dipped a spoon into his patch-stew when it came.

Ludwig Grün – a card player – said, 'Excuse Conrad, Herr Bauss. A bullet ploughed a groove in his skull. It has a metal plate in it, but he's not right.'

Lappsuppe meant chopped up odds and ends; cubes of meat, bits of sausage, vegetables and potatoes, all very wholesome. Tomorrow – Friday – only lentil soup would be available.

'Conrad and I were called up in forty-one. From the train, we saw the tower of the Bartholomäuskirche pass and said, "Do you think we'll see that again?"'

Despite keeping an eye open, Bauss had not seen *Goneril* leave number two.

'And Conrad nearly didn't,' appended Stephan Dübner, 'but that shooting happened not on the battle-field, but out beyond Edstedt.'

Sabine brought Bauss a cognac and a bone wrapped in newspaper. 'With the compliments of Herr Langenbeck.'

Dogs were uncommon, since no one had any food to spare.

'Bribing a police dog? Isn't that an offence?' Grün asked poker-faced.

'He's not a police dog,' Bauss smiled.

'And the bones you chew are hypothetical?'

'No, real. Criminal. Not always obvious, but often expository.'

*   *   *   *

In the barrack block which stood in the grounds of the château, Uta bathed her lip and swabbed out her nostrils, whilst peering at herself in the mirror.

She resolved not to be cowed. She would go out as usual on Thursday evenings to netball practice at the Rosa Luxemburg Sporthalle. She was in the local team. Her indented figure and long dark brown hair, not unenhanced by a black gym-slip on top of a blue short-sleeved top, had perhaps helped her selection.

She set off through the cold night air, carrying a bag of PT kit and wearing her police uniform simply because it was warm.

As she neared the tram depot on Triftstrasse, with its small clock-tower and quaintly ornate stone arches, she saw a girl remonstrating with three *Vopos*. It was her team captain, Stephanie Wiesen.

The *Vopos*, on foot patrol, had stopped her and searched her bag. Apart from her netball rig they had unearthed a joint of bacon and were asking where she had obtained it.

Uta stopped, looked at the four faces and asked if she could assist.

The double-chinned Sergeant eyed the newcomer with a hint of resentment. 'We have orders to stop anyone walking alone and search them for anti-government posters.'

As Uta turned toward him, enough light fell on her face for him to see her nose and lip which had now become indigo and swollen. Between the puffy left eyelids, he glimpsed blood under the conjunctiva.

The Corporal averted her face from this inspection and asked Stephanie for her version of events. She confirmed that they had gone through her bag and found this cut of bacon. She added with a degree of conviction, that she had just bought it at the H.O. store.

The *Vopos* smirked slightly as they sensed her nervousness.

In this topsy-turvy society, those with merit and integrity were the nobodies, whilst the liars and the bent were the holders of power.

'But you were looking for posters, not bacon?' Uta cited.

'True Comrade, but if we come upon something suspicious, it is our duty to ... '

'What evidence is there Oberwachtmeister, that this bacon is illegal?' She looked at the greeny-yellow-clad male officers, suggesting that the ball was now in their court, for she knew they wanted to confiscate it.

Uta's position was ambiguous. The Border and Security Police were considered superior to the People's Police, yet she was not their boss. They were in the arena of diplomacy.

The Sergeant too, disliked having his authority undermined. He hedged. 'We're also not convinced that she is who she says she is. Her ID card has been soaked in coffee.'

'We play netball together and I can affirm that she is Stephanie Wiesen.'

Stephanie reproduced her ID and Uta eyed the stained and dog-eared tag. 'This is damaged but still valid.'

The Sergeant gave her a grudging half-smile. 'Very well.'

'Thank you, Sergeant. So you need detain Fräulein Wiesen no longer?'

The *Vopos* shuffled off. When they were out of earshot, a coarse laugh erupted from them.

Stephanie leant back against the salt-streaked russet bricks of the tram shed. 'Thank you,' she said simply. 'The bacon doesn't have the H.O. ink-mark stamped on its rind, but they missed that.'

'Don't overestimate them. They're not so bright.' Uta's opinion was drowned out by one of the town's trams rattling into the depot for the night.

Above the small cone of maroon roof-tiles which surmounted the clock-tower like a witch's hat, a thin bronze weather-vane squeaked. The clock hands showed a quarter past six.

'Come on.' Uta took her team-mate's elbow. 'We're late.'

*   *   *   *

In *Der Alte Essbacher*, Herr Langenbeck was cooking waffles on a hot cast-iron plate, using one ladleful of batter mix per waffle. Eaten with blueberry jam and sour cream they were a rare treat.

Stephan Dübner, a tin soldier with a stiff leg and a stick, reminisced. 'In forty-five, our train to Frankfurt was bombed, so we set off on foot along the embankment, through snow and leaning into a strong wind ... ' He demonstrated this by holding his right forearm at an angle.

'At Rodinghausen, in Pfuff's Billiard Hall we cooked waffles ... '

Sabine cleared a table and pocketed the tip of three one Pfennig coins.

A faint light glimmered in the Lyskirchen's flat.

A cart with worn gold lettering, stood limbered up to a dray horse. This solid nag had a rug on its back and a nose-bag.

Rüdiger Seydler, a youngish fellow, dipped a biscuit into his gritty coffee, then abandoning the crossword in *Neues Deutschland*, came over to Bauss.

Pointing to a seat, he asked, 'May I?'

Bauss waved a hand.

'You are the oldest officer in the *Grenzpolizei*, Herr Bauss?'

'If you mean "most senior", then "yes".'

'Sorry. I live in a flat in Malabar Terrasse ... '

'Terrace-houses, but spacious ones ... middle-class once?'

'Yes. Well, a fellow I think from Berlin ... '

Isolde left their tenement.

'Sorry. I have to go.'

The Chief of Police leapt up, put down ten Marks and pulling on his coat, stumbled towards the door.

Wearing her usual faded blue coat, she carried her violin and basket.

He set off in the direction she had taken. Then, just when he thought he had lost her, he saw a knot of people outside the Bartholomäuskirche and a sign-board advertising a concert.

* * * *

Torsten Goitschel lived in the flat opposite the Lyskirchens.

It had faded curtains and a wooden sofa, heavy but with soft pale gold cushions.

He sat pencilling a note on an eighteenth-century Russian elegy, written after the then in-vogue Italian pattern. Beside him lay a pre-1917 history book, in which kings and knights had yet to be blackened or replaced by Luddites and murderers, recast as 'philosophers' or 'philanthropists'.

He was a reader at the University, a scholar in whom any worldly ambition would seem to be past hope of fulfilment.

Someone tapped gently on his door, a student or an acquaintance perhaps?

He opened it and saw a tall, classy, yet hard-nosed woman of about thirty. He gave her a question-mark smile.

'Herr Goitschel?'

'Yes.'

'I'm Fräulein Stege. May I?'

He ushered her in, though a little bemused.

'I'm here on semi-official business.'

He noted the tan briefcase. Also she seemed quite self-assured, an unusual quality in East Germany, where no one could feel too sure of their ground.

Turning on her heel, she showed him her State Police warrant card, then indicated the coffee-table and sofa. 'Could we?'

'If you wish.'

He eyed her oval face with its dark mole and they sat down.

'I want us to have an informal but practical discussion.'

'Does that mean that you talk and I listen?'

She smiled. 'No, the other way round.'

He was in his mid-forties, his face quite smooth and youthful, though it had the speech and habits of an older man.

They were sat well apart and she crossed her legs. 'You talked today on the telephone with one Sophie Höh?'

'I did.'

She nodded awkwardly. 'I think you might be able to help us; to reveal pieces of gold?'

'Gold? Figuratively, I trust?'

'Or literally if you prefer. Tell me, were you and Sophie Abwehr agents?'

'Abwehr agents? In the war? Not at all. We were code-breakers.'

An empty toast rack pushed to one side, the dregs of filtered coffee and some crumbs on a linen napkin, prompted her to ask, 'A late breakfast?'

'An early tea. I had a fresh egg, so I poached it.'

She tried a cautious smile. 'I've been sent from Berlin, yet my purpose is not strictly official.'

'I can't say I'm any clearer.'

'We are trying to find something, something hidden late on in the war.'

'Papers? Money?'

'Perhaps.'

'Perhaps?'

'Or the equivalent.'

'And you think I may hold the key to your search?'

She felt herself to be on rocky ground. 'What do you know about the shooting out at Rohrdorf in 1944?'

'The what?'

106

'My name's Luise.' Why the hell had she said that?

'There must be some mix-up here, some crossed wires.'

Her medium brown hair lay plaited in a ring on the back of her head. Roman maidens are often so depicted. Her narrow nostrils were in keeping with her thin face.

He perceived in her a veiled fragility. Her loftiness was artificial. Yet also he felt sympathy for her. 'Miss Stege – er, I mean Luise – would you like coffee?'

She hesitated. 'Thank you.' This had to be preferable to the lonely Hotel Lindeneck.

Standing up, she shed her nicely-tailored three-quarter length bluey-green coat and her green neckerchief and hung them over the arm of the sofa.

They went to the kitchen recess, where he filled the kettle and lit the gas.

From the quality of her sage-green skirt, cream blouse, apple green cardigan, white stockings and pointed black shoes, Torsten knew that she had high-level connections.

Sitting down again on the sofa, he patted the spot beside himself and invited her to rejoin him.

'Do you want me to sit right beside you?'

'No, I was just beating the dust out of the cushion.'

Again she hesitated, but then smiled and sat down stiffly a mere inch from him. She said to herself, 'This is crazy.'

Both had experienced little of human intimacy. Both enjoyed being independent and yet …

They viewed one another like rare coins of uncertain value. The kettle whistled.

He made the coffee, found some cake and resumed his place.

'You're quite old-fashioned,' she said, wishing to elicit a reaction.

'Antique?'

'Hmm ... antiques are valuable.'

'I rest my case.' He suppressed a grin. 'Tell me about this Rohrdorf escapade?'

'I know extremely little about it ... only that it happened and that something worth a lot of money is thought to have been hidden nearby.'

His hand touched hers. She retracted it, but gently.

'Hearsay says that it rained and the red ink ran on the wooden boxes.'

'What wooden boxes?'

'Someone called Conrad said, "That signifies blood. Some of us will die."'

'At Rohrdorf?'

She looked at him with anticipation. He seemed sincere, unpretentious, authentic. She took his hand.

He lifted hers and kissed it. 'I often dream of Spartan maidens, but that is just folly ... unless you are one?'

'I think their skirts were shorter ... Torsten.'

* * * *

The Bartholomäus Church was Lutheran and so had plain white walls and a simple beech cross which stood on a starched white altar cloth.

Bauss bought a ticket for twenty Pfennigs and stood at the back, though there were empty seats.

The choir opened with *As our Saviour came to thee,* by Wagner.

In 1932 Bauss had gone to work at a mine in the Czechoslovakian Erzgebirge Mountains, but had via a friend, heard that Susanne had married.

The town possessed a highly gifted contralto who sang *Art thou troubled? Music shall comfort*, from Handel's opera *Rodelinda*. She wore a flared orange dress with that classical Greek box-like border in grey above its hem.

The Police Chief stretched his neck and glimpsed Isolde amid the string players, with her violin tucked under her chin and the slender white fingers of her right hand arched round the heel of her bow.

This aria spoke not of swans, forests and moonlight as in the more magical pieces by the romantics, but it had a simple if muted dramatic charm.

From a chance encounter near the end of the war, he had learnt Susanne's married name. Lyskirchen is very uncommon and – as if fate were teasing him – he found her eventually under his very nose here in Essbach.

After a chorus from Bellini's *I Puritani* came the interval with coffee and biscuits in the north transept. Lorenz found himself amongst people whom he did not know, but Gerfried the sexton – seeing his isolation – joined him and made polite conversation.

Suddenly Bauss realised he was behind Isolde. He felt his body change; drained of futility as by the presence of a deity.

Though winsome, she was not sensuous. Her unawareness of her own body's appeal precluded that.

Lorenz drifted off and peered at her violin and bow lying on a chair. Her violin was a Storioni, but as that made it moderately valuable – in fact the most valuable thing she owned – she had removed the label from inside it.

As the audience resumed their seats, he left unobtrusively, went to where he had parked the old – and once luxurious – Horch and sat in it.

The previous Lutheran pastor had boldly denounced elements of their State doctrine. When asked to withdraw these remarks, he had said, 'You are building on sand and at some point your system will collapse.' He had been shot in the yard of the local prison, but it was the work of the *Volkspolizei*, whose ogre-like chief oscillated between the pathological and the neurotic.

He thought of the knight Tannhäuser, who on meeting the pure and pious Elisabeth, had wished to abandon his pagan and sensual ways, be absolved and begin a transformed life.

Two lovers leant against his car, kissing and fondling, until he rapped on the window.

Isolde, passionless and unassuming, had not preened herself like the curvy bassoon player. She seemed content with our old, everyday and innocent earth. She had no desire for the fabulous or the extraordinary.

Soon she would go home through the narrow Uhrmachergasse. Dare he do something? A tangle of resentment and fantasy beat at his heart's door.

But … this usually reliable old motor refused to start.

*   *   *   *

The iron bedstead creaked as they slithered about between its chilly sheets.

Lying on his side, Udo pressed his forehead against Greta's, mimicking a playful stag.

She imagined his penis to be an incendiary firework which would kindle the furnace of her body.

Their frenzied sexual writhings intensified. An implacable compulsion drove her forwards until with a short loud gasp she paused. Was anyone else in his blacked-out pen?

He made a pitch for a fourth foray, but she refused. 'No.'

He tried again.

'I said "No."'

He shrugged and turned onto his stomach.

Greta forced her teeth together so as not to scream at the demons lurking in this den.

Udo gave a yawn and tried to sleep.

He could guess what a dance she had led that poor Christoph fellow. Like a dog she would offer him a biscuit and then pat him on the head as he ate it. Then she would give him another biscuit and this time belt him when he ate it, so that the poor wretch did not know what to do to please her.

She bit her lip. 'You're not very "romantic" Udo,' she said with unconvincing casualness.

He could sense the anguish in her voice. One word he hated was 'love'. He felt he could tolerate just about anything except the question, 'Do you love me?'

'Do you think you love me, Udo?'

After gritting his teeth, he thought that love has many forms, so he answered, 'Yes.'

Her tension eased slightly and she turned onto her side again so as to face him. It was too dark for her to be able to see his expression. Wearily he tickled her again, but she showed no sign of responding.

'Do you believe in "love", Udo?'

He ignored her, unable to face being cynically euphemistic a second time.

After two more bouts, warm and sticky, they fell asleep.

Greta dreamt of her grandmother pushing knitting-needles into her breasts and saying, 'You have to say to Eitel that you're sorry. It's that easy.'

The girl had said to the silly old hag, 'I'll not kiss anyone's feet.'

She awoke, lying on her front in a pitch black room, her heart racing.

*   *   *   *

Bauss had returned to his office.

The distant drum-roll of a train penetrated the lucid winter's night. Its note changed and echoed as it went into a cutting.

He studied Uta's map of the old quarry at Rohrdorf.

Its grey roads and green forests abruptly underwent a maladjustment of focus. He laid down his ruler, leant back, loosened his tie and undid the top button of his shirt.

In Rome, the Pope had refused Tannhäuser – or Tannenhäuser – absolution believing him deep down to still hanker after his old darker delights. 'The chance of your receiving grace, is as likely as my staff here sprouting green leaves.'

Susanne's pleasant features were safely stored in his oft-darkened mind. She were not a Circassian mountain lass tending her goats. And certainly she were not Pushkin's harem girl from the Tartar stronghold of Bakhchisarai. 'No, you are my sacred and sweet, Sussi,' he frowned, 'Austrian and fickle.'

'Lorenz … take our past with a pinch of salt.'

'Its events are the truth?'

'No, especially not its events.'

Lieutenant Westenfeld knocked on his door.

'It is late Herr Oberkommissar. Can I do anything for you?'

'Oh, er … ask someone in the canteen to bring a coffee and a roll up, thank you.'

The Lieutenant bowed slightly and left.

Susanne's ghost picked up again. 'A poisoned apple killed my husband.'

'Husband? Anyway, you were Eve … colluding with the snake.'

'Very poetic.'

'The snake served you well, didn't he?'

'Ekkehard was naïve.'

'Or did he know?'

'Sometimes, we must resign ourselves … My sister sewed her wedding ring into the hem of her skirt, but still the Red Army soldiers found it and took it.'

The canteen girl came and went.

He quoted Catullus; 'I hate and I love. Why do I do this, you ask? I know not, but it happens and I am tortured.'

*   *   *   *

Returning to her barrack block, Corporal Dietl passed the spot where Thilo had been shot. She cut a sprig of holly –

with red berries – off a bush in someone's garden and laid it there.

The ex-Luftwaffe two-storey accommodation had been built when the château had been requisitioned for trainee radio operators in the late thirties.

She flipped on the light-switch to the toilet, but a shout from within indicated that she had in fact turned it off. She flicked it back on. Private Neumann came out. 'It's your fault if the floor's wet.'

Uta refused to smile.

'By the way, you had a visitor about an hour ago. Sergeant Bauer came with a blonde woman … slightly buxom. They searched your room.'

'Why?'

'She found an electric fire hidden in your kitbag.' It was against regulations to use electricity without permission and this would most likely merit disciplinary action.

Uta knew that the State respected no one's privacy, but this was a police establishment. 'What did she say?'

'She asked if it explained your singed blanket?'

'Who was she anyway?'

'The Sergeant will have recorded her name. All he whispered to me was *"Staatspolizei"*.'

In the upstairs kitchen, Corporal Dietl boiled water and made a glass of hot blackcurrant drink.

She peered out of the window. The remnants of the Italian garden were visible in the weak rays of a street-light. Its untended yews had long since grown wild. The archipelago of water lilies in the pond though had survived despite clumps of invading weed. A screen of snowy elms and a high stone wall separated them from the tannery.

She put the light on in her room. Had her unnamed visitor searched for something specific; banknotes for instance?

The grey steel bed, the grey steel wardrobe, the table, lamp and chair were all ex-Luftwaffe.

Sitting on the edge of her bed, she went through a box of magazines, books and pamphlets. It was not unknown for something incriminating to be planted.

What if Joos came in the night? Should she sleep with her pistol under her pillow? Or put the wardrobe against the door? Or should she leave a rolled up mat under the blankets as in *Jack the Giant Killer*? He could shag that instead.

Thilo's lanky form appeared to her. His voice had had a very nasal quality. His own name when he pronounced it sounded like, 'tobbtobb'.

She said a short prayer and went to bed.

*   *   *   *

Torsten rested an arm behind Luise's shoulders.

'Stege is an unusual name. There's the Minister for Railways, but … '

'Werner Stege. I'm his niece.'

'Oh. No doubt he carries a lot of weight?'

'His desk does. It has stone supports with a solid oak board on top and mountains of paper.'

He fingered the nape of her neck. 'But that's the kennel. What about the dog?'

She thought about this. 'Hard to say, but he seems well ensconced as a part of government. Why am I telling you this?'

They kissed, a quick touch of the lips, poured the coffee and shared the slice of stale cake. He slid his fingers into her skirt's waist-band and felt … her panties.

She did not object, but eyed his stuffed bookcase. 'Are you a member of the Party?'

'No.'

'I guessed not, but your post at the University?'

'There was no one else suitably qualified.'

'Membership opens doors – literally – entry into cinemas and exemption from proscribed travel.'

'I'm sure.'

They kissed again.

'We must remember curfew,' he remarked.

'I have a pass. So what did you do in the war?'

'I was at Cuxhaven, code-breaking, in a camouflaged warehouse … easy to find as only it was camouflaged.'

'It was my uncle, who persuaded me to come to Essbach on this nutty treasure hunt.'

'Treasure … not me I take it?'

'No. Gold, but I think he had metal in mind, not academia … or tenderness.'

He undid some of her blouse's buttons, kissed her softly and touched the soft pale skin of her small sunshade-like but nicely pointed breasts. 'Neat, pointed … "perky" is the word.'

She gave him a dour smile. 'My breasts are small. Most men like them large.'

'No. That's coarse, common … It ruins the aesthetic.'

'I thought you would be beyond such thoughts?'

'Men are never beyond such thoughts.'

He drew circles on one of them.

'You're tickling me.'

'Someone found a gold block in a cellar here, some years back. It came to the metallurgy department for analysis … I think they said its trace elements were antimony, tellurium and lead, which Professor Labrosse said pin-pointed it as coming from the Western Carpathians.'

'You have a good memory.'

'And,' he added, 'that tin as another constituent, is characteristic for Transylvanian panned river-bed gold.'

She let her head fall onto his pullover-covered chest and then they seized one another.

*   *   *   *

A clock's faint chimes rang softly out over the sleeping town.

Udo awoke. He reorientated himself as to who lay beside him.

He rolled heavily onto his side and put his arms around her warm lardy flesh. She was too still. This told him that she were awake.

'What do you want?'

'I was just seeing if you're warm … and content.'

'That sounds like false solicitousness.'

What was she blathering about? A bull had served her. Her wish had been fulfilled.

'Thank you for the theatre trip,' she said with forced bonhomie.

'Tell me about your other boyfriends, Greta.'

'You're not jealous?'

He repressed an incipient yawn.

'One was an athlete. Plenty of muscle, but a bore … '

'And you were a whore?' thought Udo.

'Then, Christoph … he was so unsure though.'

'Very understandable,' thought Eckman, again to himself.

'I think he's looking for a saint.'

Udo pulled a face in the darkness.

'He'll end up as a bottle-washer … no ambition.'

Feeling like another bout of sex, Udo squeezed himself more firmly against her flank.

She turned onto her back, ready to reciprocate in their common need.

As the climax subsided, a bell rang in Eckman's head; a remark by Niehaus. He kissed Greta's nose and clutched one of her breasts. 'This Christoph fellow, does he have a sister called Isolde?'

'Yes. They live in Keplerstrasse.'

'What's she like?'

Their probable link with the posters crossed her mind.

Udo drew designs on her moist back.

'She's a bit pale and pasty. Meticulous … often bent over a sheet of score paper transposing a horn part or something.

Why should she interest you?'

'It's only a rumour … but there's a need for police vigilance. Woodworm can bring a house down.'

'I can't see her as a risk.'

'It's not only braggarts who spread trouble.'

'No. "Bags of discipline, the more the better." That was my father's motto,' said Greta.

The cloud-cover had cleared and the quarter-moon

shone unexpectedly into the bedroom. It peeped in at the bed and the a heap of blankets topping the two sated bodies. They were awake and lying on their sides, their bodies touching but their minds a light-year apart.

*   *   *   *

Lorenz Bauss had been born in Coburg in 1908.

In his early childhood he had dug holes in the garden near the apple tree. He had had a wooden toy tipper lorry and would lie on his side for hours with bits of slate and wood making roads and tunnels and mines.

His widowed mother believed in hardiness and independence. They spent long hours tending their rows of vegetables and took gruelling weekend walks. She did not make him feel that women might be kind or gentle.

In 1927 he moved to Munich to study mining engineering.

1929 was the year of his besottedness. He saw her one April morning in a café and she instantly evoked a heady and peculiar quiver in him, quite unlike any previous attraction.

She had had a good shape and shortish blonde hair and her straw boater had hung on a cord behind her shoulders. He recalled her giggling softly with her friend. One of her most appealing traits was her ability to be daft without being crude.

Susanne Dettmann at sixteen, was five years his junior. Her father practised as a surgeon in Innsbruck and she had come to Munich to train as a nurse.

After her friend left, he had raised his hat and asked if she would walk with him to the Hofgarten to hear the band play. She had seemed only mildly taken aback and was courteous in her reply. Being still so young, she may have felt a trifle flattered, but her refusal was firm if gentle. She had touched his cuff and said that she had to attend a lecture. None the less, he felt so ecstatic that he had been brave enough to try. He loved everything about her so so deeply.

He tried to dress more smartly, to work hard and to deny all impure thoughts for her sake.

He yearned for her every moment and felt an unwavering conviction that she, after she had recognised these same puzzling emotions and reconciled them in her own breast, would reciprocate.

Yet his further approaches were consistently resisted. Did it vex her that her adulthood's purpose should be to make this absurd fellow shine through the sweetness of her love?

But whereas his impassioned hopes would not allow him to live decently without her, it seemed that she could manage without him.

From then on no pleasure ever properly satisfied him. Brightness was denied. Darkness constantly knocked at the door.

And this unfulfilled amour, this shadow of paradise, it refused to budge.

But now he was haunted by a second tormentor. Her daughter seemed to censure his very existence.

Seen through the prism of his mind, she had come to avenge her father's death.

He had – crazily and wrongly he now saw – wanted to 'accidentally' run her down.

Suddenly she stood in front of him. 'You want to do away with me, Lorenz? To roll me up in your lovely pink carpet?'

'Go and float on a cloud.'

'But not your cloud of green smoke?'

Once he had returned to the hospital dining-room in Munich to sit on a chair Susanne had sat on.

She had shipwrecked his life.

He grasped the telephone's rotary switch with his left hand and turned it to position 6 with his right, the duty officer's post. He lifted the ear-piece. 'Come up to my office.'

He stood up and wandered to the window. The flag-pole caught in the glare of an arc lamp, had had its flag lowered at dusk. The flag of the German Democratic Republic was then the same horizontal black red and yellow stripes as that used by West Germany. The gold dividers were added later.

A tattoo of knocks sounded on his door.

He sat down. 'Come in.'

Lieutenant Westenfeld entered. 'Herr Oberkommissar?'

'There's a girl I want a watch putting on.'

'Sir?'

'We still lack evidence of her scheming.'

'Are we looking for real charges or false ones?'

'A good question.'

'I try to avoid stupid ones, Sir.'

'Yes, well, you're redeeming yourself. We have just one lead … '

The Oberkommissar halted in mid-sentence. An unpleasant squeezing sensation gripped his chest. A pallor tinged his furrowed face. Drops of glistening sweat broke out on his brow. 'Oh … my chest.'

Westenfeld came round the desk unbidden, loosened Bauss's collar and unclasped his belt, before setting the telephone's rotary switch to 1 for the Guard Room and lifting the ear-piece.

This old 'house' system had seven extensions and you could obtain the one you wanted directly.

'Viktoria? Herr Bauss is unwell. Ring for an ambulance.'

The Guard Room had the external line.

CHAPTER SIX

The stars twinkle above Essbach, such loveliness and splendour encircling such pain and suffering. The town is silent now. Curfew fell an hour ago.

Life under its roofs unfolds with a leaden humdrum inevitability, whilst I, the Good Spirit, watch.

Underneath though, many fathoms down in the mould of the human heart, trolls spin shapes and angels sing of peace on earth. Deep in the dark labyrinthine womb of sleep, the infinite memory of the past evokes the things to come. And all is written with an iron stylus in the Book of Deeds.

The night is upon our players. Their fleeting joys and the dread dregs of agony rax their hearts; touches of gaiety vie with forebodings close to the brink of moral anarchy.

And regard for us – the deities of the old dispensation – has gone. Yet still we watch and guard.

*   *   *   *

Isolde lay in her narrow bed, the blankets up to her chin.

Though her parents had always been kind to one another, she had sensed – since as young as five – that they were somehow play-acting.

In the hamlet of Ebbkirch, on the eastern border of Germany, on a balmy March day in 1945, an elderly schoolmaster had taught his three remaining pupils.

Outside, although the birds sang, the farmhouses and orchards had lain silent.

As a bar of sunlight caught a swirl of chalk particles from the blackboard duster, they heard the squeak of brakes.

Three youths in ragged clothes clambered over a lorry's tail-board as the schoolmaster – Herr Hauff – with Frederica, Gerda and Isolde came out of the school-house.

The driver, in a torn field-grey uniform, spotted a chicken pecking at some straw and made a grab for it, but to the glee of the girls it zig-zagged off in a trail of dust.

Frederica drew up water from the cast-iron pump. Its linchpin squeaked. Its initial silt-tinctured squirts she let run into the stone trough. Herr Hauff raided their store of apples and soon they all sat on a wall, munching and drinking.

Gerda asked the driver – one Lorenz Bauss – why he had a sticking plaster on his nose?

'Well, last night, driving without lights, we ran into an elk.'

'Oh, a sweet furry elk? Was it hurt?'

'Schoolgirls … ' One boy shook his head.

Isolde had been sent there to work on a farm.

The newcomers rested in an empty barn until dusk, when all helped to organise a make-shift meal. Two candles burnt on the desks in the school-room, which had been pushed together. On a wooden platter stood a loaf of rough black bread – made mostly from husks – and a mouldy cheese which Herr Hauff had acquired two days before by bartering his son's bicycle for it. Bauss brought a bag from his cab with some tomatoes and boiled potatoes.

In the intimate half-light of the candles, they were as on an island, surrounded by dark forests and bogeymen … and possibly Russians.

Later, Bauss – preparing to sleep in a hayloft – thought of Isolde. Her diffident though erect form, in an everyday blouse and worn black skirt and her face in particular, had reminded him of Susanne.

For breakfast there were only more apples, though Frederica popped a sly peppermint drop into her mouth.

Erich saw her slip it in behind her large front teeth. 'Can I have one?'

'No.'

'*Bellissima*?'

'No!'

'Decibel-*issima*?'

Gerda laughed.

'Oi. Whose side are you on?'

Erich offered a bent Turkish coin.

'No.'

Bauss ignoring this, silently observed Isolde's *à la Titus* coiffure – hair tied up in a loose sheaf – which had begun to unravel.

'Isolde, may I ask your mother's maiden name?'

'Dettmann,' she had answered simply.

'So you *are* Sussi Dettmann's daughter?'

'Yes,' she replied, with slightly widened eyes.

War is said to throw up strange coincidences. 'I knew your mother … when she was a student nurse in Munich.'

She gave him an unintentionally beatific smile.

Was there a dismissive artfulness about her too?

Erich watched Frederica, whilst Hauff studied his lecherous and ugly form. He had that arrogance which can be oddly attractive to women.

'Why are you peering at me?' Frederica queried.

'I wasn't. I was just staring into space ... though I suppose it's the same thing.'

'Oh, get lost.'

In medieval Germany, when a farmer and his men sat down to eat, only the master or the leading hand could speak. The men could answer but not initiate discussion. That deeply devout world had gone.

Then they heard the gruff sounds of another vehicle drawing up, but their revived apprehension eased when they heard orders being issued in German.

*   *   *   *

A whiff of carbolic acid tinged the air. Earlier the cleaning girl had added phenol to her bucket of warm water, turning it cloudy, before mopping the stone floor. The brass door handles were beautifully polished too.

Lorenz Bauss lay in the one-bed cubicle at the end of the male ward in the town's hospital. Lights-out had been at eight o'clock – nearly two hours since – so only the faint low-voltage accumulator-fed night-lights glimmered, giving just enough light for the nurses on their ghostly rounds to mark a pulse rate say on a graph on the clipboard which hung on the foot of each bed.

His pain had subsided with the shot of morphine. His metal-framed bed though had a hard lumpy mattress, not designed it seemed to encourage long stays.

Her limpid image, first seen in Ebbkirch with its obscured effulgence, appeared once more, backed by clouds either charcoal-grey or with the silvery dullness of molten lead. Isolde again debarred him from sleep.

Outside the wind howled.

Heidi, the junior night nurse, came in quietly. She was tall and slim.

'Has the morphine worn off, Herr Bauss?'

'More or less. I have only a very mild ache now.'

She shone a pen-torch at his face. 'You look a better colour too.'

The whites of his eyes showed them swivelling towards her. Her dark sharp sand-glass outline in its neat uniform made her pungently enticing.

'You have a lovely shape, Heidi.'

'Thank you. *You* need to lose some weight.'

'Its all round my midriff. I have six pairs of trousers hung up at home, all with increasing waist sizes.'

'Try buying the elasticated type.'

'Then I might expand indefinitely?'

She gave a willowy smile.

'The transition from biconcave to biconvex.'

Like a child with a bag of sweets, Bauss always liked the girl in the prettiest wrapper.

Her uniform consisted of a white and grey narrow-striped and slightly flared dress, a starched white pinafore and an elasticated belt with a chrome clasp.

She flicked the mercury downwards in the thermometer which had stood in a vial of antiseptic and popped it under his tongue.

He watched her oval carved-ivory face and her curved eye-lashes, yet her task unfortunately was the alleviation of pain, not the giving of delight.

She examined the thermometer and marked his temperature on the chart. She counted his pulse whilst peering down at the fob-watch which was pinned to the top edge of her apron, raising it from its resting position on the shallow cone of her left breast.

He said nothing, yet he had a feeling.

She departed with slight dance-like or sinusoidal movements of her body, deftly stroking his harp strings of desire.

*   *   *   *

A fraught S.A. warrant officer entered the school-house.

Oberwachtmeister Lehmann stamped on the dusty boards and spoke of their snap enlistment with both intensity and a speech impediment.

'A bit theatrical,' whispered Gerda.

'Almost a comedy,' came Frederica's *sotto voce* reply.

He glowered at the tall Frederica. '*If* the Bolsheviks win, you idiots will finally understand what this was all about.'

She kept her face straight. 'So, what's the master plan?'

'Children above ten are no longer *hors de combat*.'

'Oh.'

He gave an impromptu 'sit-rep' on the surrounding military dispositions. He was as out of touch with reality as Hitler was in his bunker, issuing impossible commands to non-existent troops. 'Fourteenth Panzer Division to advance northwards.' No one dared tell him that it had already been annihilated.

Somewhere some chairs fell over.

'What's that? Is someone breaking in?' snapped Lehmann.

'Or breaking out?' muttered Frederica in an undertone.

Wearing a yellow arm-band, stamped with the letters 'VS', an old fellow entered bearing an armful of obsolete rifles. There were eight rounds of ammunition per rifle.

After ten minutes of instruction, they moved off into the cool evening air.

A lingering semi-circle of cerise light expanded in the darkening sky to the East.

'Star shell,' remarked Bauss, 'but not ours. Ours is more yellowy.'

'Magenta,' observed Isolde. 'Very pretty.'

'Magenta?' Frederica queried. 'What a word. Lehmann would be struggling with pink.'

They passed the outlines of barns. Some apple trees had had a strip of bark cut out two-thirds of the way round their trunks, so sensing death, they would bear more fruit this autumn.

Between a coppice and a pasture, they descended toward the darkly reflective and eyot-dotted River Issl. To their right a gravelled track led to a vapour-obscured broken bridge.

They were to guard the ford, so they lay down on the reverse slope of a bank with their rifles.

Isolde had no brown 'Land Service' uniform as there were none spare, so she wore her patched school clothes with a cuff-band which read 'Landdienst' in Gothic letters.

A bittern gave a booming cry. Gerda said, 'They live amid the rushes and as camouflage, have vertical brown stripes.'

'A country girl,' observed Bauss, who lay next to Isolde in this cordon of pickets. 'Where is your mother now?' He tried to sound neutral.

'In Emmendingen, near Freiburg. At least that's the last I heard.'

*　　*　　*　　*

Joos reached the flat in Malabar Terrasse soon after ten.

In Thilo's cramped kitchen, he lit the stove and made coffee, all with his left arm, his right one being in a sling.

He examined the rip in the side of his coat. And where was that wad of money? Had it fallen out of this torn pocket? How could one thorn do all this?

Luise had dropped him off at the infirmary. Night admissions were, he then discovered, via a rear entrance in Lazarettgasse. Cradling his painful limb, he had walked there through a pall of oily smoke. Some kids had found a wartime distress flare and instead of aiming it upwards, had fired it into a hedge, where with a fierce red flame it gave off greasy hydrocarbon particles. Joos was dotted with spots.

He had sat in the examination room, brightly lit, aseptic and tiled in cream with trolleys of instruments and a blue and terracotta Roman mosaic floor. The night sister wore a grey dress and a white pinafore with a red cross on it.

'I think I've dislocated my shoulder.'

She viewed his dirty face. 'So not a case of black spotted fever?'

What a martinet. But then she smiled.

As she eased off his coat and pullover, he had barely restrained a howl. She compared sides.

The duty house-surgeon was summoned and with the

head of his humerus manipulated back into its socket and his arm in a sling, he left.

Thilo Hengel's flat was one half of the ground floor of a house which had once belonged to the Stehrs.

He and Luise had searched it minutely, peering into holes, under cupboards and lifting floor-boards. They had found a school exercise book with 'L. Stehr' on its cover and a packet of photographs, but nothing more.

Balthasar Axt had worked in the Reich Treasury during the war and seen the signals on this alleged Rohrdorf 'incident'. The Reichsbank had the stock records of Romania's gold. Bars were stored in wooden boxes, five to a box. He had substantiated all the arithmetic. An extra sixteen boxes had disappeared just before the Red Army arrived.

Joos had recently set up accounts for the five of them – using aliases supported by forged passports obtained by Stege – with a small bank in Göttingen in anticipation of success.

He and Luise had intended to interview the fellow upstairs this evening, but where the devil was she?

He went up alone, knocked and the tortoise-like head of Rüdiger Seydler peeped round his door.

Joos showed his warrant and was admitted. They sat down.

'I need your help, Herr Seydler,' Joos began pleasantly. 'It's about the family who lived here ten years back.'

'The Stehrs?'

'Yes. Did you ever meet them?'

'No. The local commune took the house over in 1946 and divided it up.'

Rüdiger had been in bed since eight, the stove had died and the dingy room was icy cold.

'The woman was called Ingrid and the boy Lothar. There might have been a girl too?'

'The husband had died in forty-four?'

'No one mentioned him.'

'So, the mother and children? Where did they go?'

'The butcher, across the road, says they escaped to the West … to Oldenburg.'

Joos showed him the photographs. Places and dates had been scribbled on their backs. 'Are these the Stehrs?'

'They're the right age.'

One – presumably snapped by the mother – read; 'Erwin Greta and Lothar – Rohrdorf 1938.' They were picnicking on a curiously shaped rock beside a railway signal post.

A rubber-encased clock – a shock-proof type for use in tanks – stood on a shelf. Russian soldiers stole and sold such things.

'Where did you acquire that clock?'

'At the market.'

'It's an offence to receive stolen goods.'

'I didn't know it was stolen. I'll be as helpful as I can, Sir.'

'Don't worry … I can pretend I didn't see it. Look, have you any papers left by the Stehrs … anything?'

'Er, no … only a rumour.'

'Oh?'

'Some say that Ingrid was the daughter of a Count from Lower Saxony. The Count and the Countess died of cholera whilst visiting Palestine in 1922, so that Ingrid and her twin brother – who had just attained their majority –

inherited the estate. It is believed that they were incestuous and with the parents gone, became less discreet about it.'

'They could now sleep together in the château?'

'I suppose so. In 1925 they were arrested in Vienna, dressed in each other's clothes.'

Joos took a deep breath. 'After our defeat in the first war, a lot of secret traits floated to the surface.'

'Well, the brother was locked up in an asylum, but the girl skipped bail and disappeared.'

'And that's Ingrid, who then married Erwin Stehr? What was her original name?'

'Johanna von Geisberg.'

'Hmm.'

'The butcher says that she pronounced the initial "st" of a word as "st" and not "sht", which suggests a north German upbringing.'

Joos thought for some seconds. Detective stories always contain both genuine clues and red herrings. 'That is all quite colourful, but does it actually help me? I'll think it over. But thank you.'

The butcher was a cheerful if overweight fellow.

'When her husband was away in the army, I used to serve her.'

'You were lovers?'

'Well, I wouldn't exactly put it like that. There's a girls' ditty isn't there?

"She who needs it, sense she spurns,

When it's over, sense returns."'

Joos smiled. 'I've not heard that before. Anyway, she went to Oldenburg you think?'

'Yes, but moved on to Amsterdam around 1950.'

'You're very well informed?'

'She sent me a post-card … the local police interviewed me about it.'

'And?'

'Well, she simply wanted the address of the local Party boss … nothing more.'

'Did you reply?'

'They told me not to.'

He stood up and rummaged in an old dresser.

The card showed a picture of the Vondelpark. Its cramped writing included a return address.

'Can I take this?'

The butcher screwed up his face. 'You couldn't give me something for it, Sir? I'm struggling a bit.'

Joos for once felt well-disposed. He found a twenty -Mark note and a few alcohol vouchers.

'A policeman *and* a gentleman.'

The injury to his shoulder had humbled him a little and this in turn had led to his extracting more from his interviewees than by his usual rougher tactics.

Back in Thilo's flat, he reflected that he had at last made some progress.

He re-examined his coat. It was unbelievable. That overbold police witch, was going to suffer for this.

* * * *

Isolde's blankets tickled her nose. Existence then was not simply drifting like some rebel comet … as her sojourn in Ebbkirch had also proven.

'Does your mother still nurse?' Bauss had probed.

'She stopped when she bore me.'

'I worked in mines in Czechoslovakia ... ores of silver, manganese.'

She had ignored this.

Love he had learnt, is about suffering.

Frederica and Lehmann had dragged fallen branches forwards, to steady their rifles on. Sprays of hawthorn twigs with white-green shoots further hid their positions.

Despite the midnight hour, they had felt clear-headed and awake.

The moon glinted on the treacly water. Lehmann had rigged up a trip-wire beyond the ford. A string at knee-height had a cluster of empty sardine tins tied to either end.

An old culvert nearby had a peaty smell. Its bricks were uneven and lumpy having been hand-moulded and baked a century before. 'Somewhere to hide?' murmured Gerda.

Pink spiral nebulae dotted the blue-black sky above the dark fir-trees. All seemed deceptively tranquil.

Then to the south, heavy guns boomed. Pale-edged grey flashes were seen; the bleached stones of the track were glimpsed fitfully.

The sardine tins jangled. Then silence. Had a rabbit triggered the trip-wire? Like medieval maidens, they listened intently as for the hoof-beats of their loved one's horse.

The fiery erratic trajectory of a flare rose then plummeted, to land on the water where it floated, then died.

An unseen tank ground and growled.

An unexpected whoosh and a whiff of acrid smoke startled them. Then a vivid blue and amber circle of flame, a ragged explosion and a turbulent imploding ball of crimson followed. In the phosphorescent pinky-white after-glow were the burning entrails of the tank.

A shoulder-held recoilless anti-tank projectile, a *Panzerfaust* – similar to a bazooka – had scored a direct hit.

Lehmann's face gleamed with manic certitude. 'We got the bastard!'

Then a *Wehrmacht* major appeared, bellowing like a bull. These *Volkssturm* amateurs had destroyed one of their own tanks.

The sporadic, arrhythmic percussions of rifle-fire began.

*　　*　　*　　*

It was the dead of night. Uta slept.

Thilo had been moonstruck with her. His mates had told him that they had said to her how he wished to take her out and that she had replied that she would think about it. Believing this, he had approached her to fix the time and the place, but whilst she reddened, he had suddenly spotted these 'mates' doubled up in hysterics.

Bauss whispered, 'We're lucky to have you.' Beside him, the Pope's staff sprouted green leaves.

Then Joos, wearing a patched coat, tobogganed into an abyss.

She awoke. Yet what would her own future be?

All she knew was that she must be brave and up-beat. A field with golden corn ought surely one day to appear?

*　　*　　*　　*

In the high-ceilinged cream-painted cubicle, Bauss wearing a cotton night-shirt, lay propped up in bed on a pile of pillows.

Heidi came in. Her name badge, pinned onto her pinafore over her right nipple, read: 'Spitz A'. How appropriate. And the other one? 'Spitz B'?

Whilst straightening a pillow, she whispered, 'You can see me if you want to?'

So, she was not so dainty and innocent as she looked? And by gosh, did he lust for her?

Girls' tight underwear, he had heard, not only kept them narrow-waisted, but by constricting the gut and reducing its blood flow, lessened their appetites.

The spring-clip pinged as she jotted down his observations on the chart. Then she gave him a quick cuddle before a wraith-like exit.

He ran an index finger along his stubbly unshaven chin.

She had a wedding ring, but her husband was a sailor and was away.

*   *   *   *

The whiff of pine resin tinged the air. Liquid gold flowed into the charcoal furrows of the eastern sky and the plaintive cry of a moorhen pierced the halcyon silence. In Ebbkirch, dawn had broken.

A silvery mist hung over the rafts of weed in the ivy-green water of the River Issl.

Frederica and Isolde walked back to the village. Everyone else had disappeared. The front had passed them by. For them the war was over.

Isolde lay on her side, emerging as from syncope to the resounding clang of the first tram's bell as it stopped in the Luisenhof.

CHAPTER SEVEN

Udo's cramped kitchen had a pair of French windows, near which stood a tiny table and two wooden chairs.

Outside it was still dark. Falling snow had been blown against the square panes forming crescents. A forty watt light bulb cast a dim light.

In his pyjamas and three woollies, he prepared breakfast; slices of heavy grey bread, ham, plum jam and a tasteless cheese.

He muttered to himself, 'Breakfast for Madame.' He called through into the bedroom, 'Greta? How do you like your coffee?'

'Strong.'

Duly she entered in a cotton night-dress loaned to her by Udo with her old creased and scuffed brown leather coat on top, unbuttoned but with its belt loosely tied. Looking tousled, she sat down whilst her host poured the coffee.

'Cream?'

'Thanks.'

He too sat down. 'So, are policemen as black as they're painted?'

'Blacker. This is classy crockery.'

'Capodimonte, nicked I believe from the château at Dossfels.'

'I'ld like a crocodile-skin handbag.'

'They say that in America now, genetic engineering is so advanced that they can breed the baby crocs with the handles already on ... but I daresay that's just propaganda?'

'With this snow falling, it's like being on an island.' She gave him a hopeful smile.

'This afternoon – when I get home – we'll take a walk in the park … kick through the snow, feed the swans?'

He refilled their coffee cups.

'This Lyskirchen girl … you can't tie her to anything a bit dodgy?'

'She's too lacklustre to be doing anything risky.'

'Minor criminals look criminal, but major ones are often less obvious.'

A sly smile crept onto Greta's face. 'Police informants? Are they paid well?'

'Payment is proportional to the quality of the tip-offs.' He noted that she were helping herself to a fourth slice of bread, this time with cheese. 'If say I asked you to plant false evidence on Christoph, that might merit fifty or sixty Marks.'

'So much?'

Udo put his shoes and coat on, he was relieved to be escaping her company.

'I already know something.'

'Sorry? What?'

'About Christoph.'

There was a moment's silence, whilst Eckman adjusted to this unexpected turn. 'The fellow who daren't say boo to a goose?'

Her fingers fidgeted in her lap, removing some imaginary fleck from her coat.

'Well … go on.'

'He's the fellow who's printing those "Befrei Deutschland" posters.'

Udo's jaw fell. 'Are you sure?'

'Well, I've seen the printing set ... and the letters are right. It's under a loose floor-board in his attic.'

Still dazed, the best Udo could manage was, 'What a stroke of luck.'

'He doesn't know that I know.'

'Good. That's important. Is Isolde implicated?'

'They're very close. She would certainly know of it.'

'Well, I had best be off. This is dramatic stuff.' He took his wallet from a bench near the cooker. From it he extracted three ten-Mark notes and put them in front of Greta.

'If this bears fruit, there'll be more. You said you've no lectures today?'

'No.'

He had rashly said she could stay if she wished. 'Pop out and buy some vegetables will you? Here's the spare key. I should be back by mid-afternoon.' He left.

Bauss had hinted at promotion to anyone who could fix a charge on Isolde Lyskirchen.

Greta remained sat at the table for a time. Eventually she picked up the three bank-notes, slid them into her coat's inside pocket and buttoned it up: the thirty pieces of silver.

*　　*　　*　　*

'Life is a shadow of a wonderful dream,' Bauss quoted to the window.

A micro-filmed specimen treatise on cadmium isotope 106 had been used to compromise both the visiting Gisèle

Bouvier and the hapless Ekkehard Lyskirchen. Exit the thorn; the imposter.

Sieglinde, a less alluring staff nurse appeared.

'The ward round's in thirty minutes.' She pointed at the wash-basin, with its soap, flannel and razor. 'Make yourself presentable and if Doktor Tosset is satisfied, you can bath and stretch your legs.

The first rays of this, Friday the sixteenth of December, glanced off the roof of Essbach's little hospital. A wren on a bare branch outside chirruped, a cheerful little fellow. Two demure young nurses came in and remade his bed, deftly and neatly folding over the tops of the sheets.

The door opened and in came Doktor Tosset followed by Siggie with a note-book and pencil. He greeted Bauss with a professionally bright smile.

'Good morning, Doctor,' the patient answered in a more matter-of-fact tone.

Tosset wore a starched white coat over the standard white shirt, plain tie and flannels. A stethoscope dangled from his neck. He glanced at the pulse rate and temperature chart.

'Any recurrence of the pain, Herr Bauss?'

'No, Doctor.'

He asked some questions and listened to the replies with an air of scepticism, implying a deeper grasp of their significance.

Sieglinde then bent the Police Chief brusquely forward and held his night-shirt up, whilst Tosset percussed his lung fields, like a vintner tapping a barrel to decide how full it was. He then listened to his heart with the heavy cold bell of his stethoscope.

The physician furrowed his brow as a judge might, before pronouncing sentence. 'You have not suffered a heart attack. Being upset or angry can mimic the symptoms – a tightness across the chest, greyness, sweating – but it subsides with no lasting damage. So, you are discharged.' He displayed the quasi-friendly air much used by professionals. 'Avoid things which excite or agitate you, Herr Bauss.'

'I'll try, Herr Doktor. Thank you.'

When dressed and waiting in the foyer for a police vehicle to collect him, a drunkard was wheeled in on a trolley. He had a shattered elbow and a complete cylinder of skin missing from his upper arm.

His injuries baffled everyone.

Bauss guessed it. 'He has lain in a gutter with his arm out at right angles and a vehicle has driven over it.'

The houseman, the nurse and the porter all looked astounded.

Sergeant Hartwig appeared and led his Chief to the waiting car.

*　　*　　*　　*

North of Edstedt lay an ivy-engulfed and dilapidated manor, one wing gutted and blackened.

Along the avenue of planes, through the long snow-bowed grass, Corporal Dietl and Private Sommer trod.

They passed a collapsed summer pavilion and a statue of a maiden swathed in a flowing low-cut dress with folds in its drapes. This had once been a civilised garden.

Beside the main door, a small cross-shaped window had had its stained glass smashed.

Sophie, the old housekeeper answered.

Inside, on a festering Bokhara rug edged with a rotting wood-block floor and a few dry toadstools of irregular shape, she had been eating bread and sausage. The furniture was long gone.

'Is Herr von Topp in?'

'Master Tristan's gone.'

'Gone where?' asked Uta.

'A man threatened him ... and he has fled, I think.'

'To where?'

'Your guess is as good as mine.'

'We heard he'd gone,' Uta said simply. Every hamlet had its Aunt Monika.

The two officers wandered around. There were coffee beans in a grubby sack. They picked briefly at rubbish, read an old post-card, looked at a painting.

'That's Master Tristan's mother, Countess Emilia ... Polish. She died during the war.'

'Was she a bit mad?' queried Uta.

'She had a strange, rather profound air. She would laugh at what was serious and take seriously things which were funny. And at Christmas parties with red kerchiefs flying from the waist-band of her black dress, she would spin round wildly doing a mazurka.'

Sommer eyed the broken chandelier.

'Her diary entry, on the day the Master was born, read: "Barley harvest begun. Son born."'

They were only a stone's throw from Rohrdorf quarry.

'The man who threatened him, was his name Joos?'

'I don't know. He was searching for some "black blocks". He punched the Master ... and said he could be shot.'

'Black blocks?'

She looked at Uta's bruised face and shrugged.

Only Sophie and the fled Master Tristan knew of one buried treasure. In February forty-five, they had filled a metal chest with silver plate and the family's most prized possession – a gold goblet brought back from the Holy Land during the Crusades – and buried it in the wood.

As the officers left, Uta looked at the pond, half-choked with weed and with a rusting pram in it and thought, 'What has happened to our country?'

* * * *

It was snowing on the parade-ground at the Border Police H.Q. A police lorry with chains on its wheels and a grey snow-plough blade bolted to the front ends of its chassis girders was clearing the approach road.

A police car turned in, its wipers keeping segments of windscreen clear.

Sergeant Hartwig stepped out, opened a rear door and Herr Bauss clambered out, dressed in his walking-out uniform. Doors were held open for him and Baumeister – on sentry-go – saluted.

Eckman, standing in the foyer, said greasily, 'I am pleased to see you recovered, Sir.'

Bauss gave him a curt nod; a last drop from a well-squeezed lemon.

Eckman whispered, 'I've had a tip-off on the Lyskirchens, Sir.'

The Chief halted. Had the roulette wheel finally stopped on zero? 'Come up to my office in … twenty minutes.'

'Sir.'

Another girl was scrubbing the corridor today, slopping water about, as Eckman entered his own office.

He smiled broadly.

'So, how coarse was Greta?' inquired Niehaus with indifferent curiosity.

'Coarse enough.'

'What, even for you?'

Eckman waggled two fingers.

'How about compromising on your freedom? This "When I'm home, I'm home," just won't work with a decent stable sort of girl.'

'Maybe one day. But ... I've had a gold-plated tip-off.'

'On what?'

'On the Lyskirchens. Telepathy Jörg, that's the key.'

'I thought it was perseverance?'

'That was last week.'

'Anyway, watch Greta doesn't saddle you with a couple of brats so that you're trapped for the next twenty years.'

'Unlike Viktoria.'

'That might be all right actually.'

'She's a bit upper crust. Her father was a naval captain. Ask her to come and view your etchings.'

Niehaus smiled benignly.

'Anyway, the Old Man wants to see me.'

He left and went upstairs.

'Well, Eckman? What's this tip-off?'

'Sir, Christoph Lyskirchen might be the one printing the "Befrei Deutschland" posters.'

Bauss's eyes widened. 'Two birds with one stone?'

'The printing kit is allegedly under a loose floor-board in the attic … where he sleeps.'

Bauss leant back. 'Is his sister party to it?'

'She would at least know about it.'

'Is this information reliable?'

'I think so. The only proof will come by raiding the flat.'

'Quite. Right, leave me to work out a plan.'

Eckman left.

Was his secular office a mere bluff, with Isolde omnipresent, blithe as a blushing rose-hued haze at the earth's outer rim?

He blanched. 'Is it you?'

'Yes Lorenz. The strewing of our last dawn together.'

'The doctor healed me.'

'No he didn't. Vinegar and brown paper. A charade. Only God can heal you, Lorenz.'

*　　*　　*　　*

Isolde sat bent over a sheet of score paper, copying out a viola part. She wore the same old blue dress but today with a pale orange cardigan. Her canvas slippers were on the floor and her white-socked feet rested on the bar between the table's two bulbous legs.

Was anyone watching the flat? To go to the window to look, might itself appear suspicious.

Her brother came in. He removed his padded jacket, pushed back his woolly and shirt and revealed a long shallow cut on his forearm. He started washing it under the tap and it bled copiously.

Isolde came to look.

'I vaulted over a wall with broken glass on it,' he explained.

'Doing what?'

'I stuck a poster up behind the old art gallery.'

'In broad daylight?'

'I don't usually, but ... '

'We've a crêpe bandage somewhere,' she began. 'We'll put it on so that you don't spread blood everywhere.' She rooted round in a drawer and found it rolled-up. When he had brought the bleeding to a temporary stop, she wound it firmly round his forearm with her nimble fingers and tucked the end in.

'You haven't seen a letter "A" have you? There's only two in the box, not three.'

'No.'

Isolde went back to her work whilst Christoph half-filled a saucepan with water, placed it on the gas hob and lowered two eggs into it. When it started to boil, he turned over a sand-glass. He buttered some bread and put it onto a chipped plate on the table, before fetching the salt-box and two spoons.

Isolde opened the Bible and read Psalm forty-nine aloud.

Christoph lifted the boiled eggs out of the saucepan with a large spoon, whose chrome had largely worn off to reveal its underlying brass and tipped them into two wooden egg-cups.

She hit her egg round the top with her spoon and then beheaded it with the handle. The egg tasted perfect with the bread and butter and salt. How often the mundane surpasses the supposedly elevated?

Outside the wind blew. Flurries of snow left the roofs to supplement the moderate fall. She thought of Lieutenant Niehaus in the church.

She went round to her brother and knelt on the floor. She extended her arms and took hold of his palms. He knelt on the floor too, though a little bemused. They hugged one another briefly with their heads side by side and their arms around one another's shoulders. He sensed from her body's tone that she was less troubled and more balmy today.

'I'll make the coffee,' he said.

CHAPTER EIGHT

Udo Eckman found Uta writing up a short report on Grehr Manor and its missing owner.

'Ah, here you are. The Oberkommissar wants to see you.'

She let her eyelids droop to discourage any attempts at eye contact.

'Thank you, Herr Rittmeister.'

A tic had begun to afflict the muscles around Bauss's right eye.

In shirt sleeve order she stood in front of his desk, neat and attentive. So absorbed did he seem in his own thoughts, that he failed to notice her black eye, though his doughy face smiled briefly before staring critically at the ceiling.

'Tristan von Topp's old servant thinks he has fled to the West because of Herr Joos's badgering him ... about some "black blocks".'

'Yes, well never mind him for the moment. Isolde is today's objective. Scene one: we scare the brother into bolting. With him gone, we raid the flat, find the printing set and charge her.'

'The printing set?'

'She's printing the "Befrei Deutschland" posters.'

'Oh?'

'That's the plan in a nut-shell.'

'Oh.'

'She's more barbed than some of you gullibles thought.' He smiled. 'We're the "A" team ... isn't that the latest expression?'

'Not the "Eh?" team?'

He expanded with a pinch of humour. 'Uta, learn from my experience and wisdom.'

'I'll try, Sir.'

He smiled at her directly. 'Am I embarrassing you?'

'Well, you're here,' she teased.

He gave a dismissive laugh.

She saw in him a lonely life; two gold-filled teeth, a leathery face, open-pored skin on his nose and now a tic.

'A goods train leaves Halle each evening and crosses the border to Bebra. It stops at the Rohrdorf sidings to pick up wagons.

Find Christoph Lyskirchen and tell him that we know about the posters. If he wants to escape then he can stowaway on this train. There will be no border checks, no sniffer dogs *et cetera*. His sister may not go. Make sure he gets on board. If he does, ring me here and say, "The donkey's gone to market," or if not, "The donkey's stayed at home." Is that clear?'

The Berlin blonde at the telephone exchange flashed through his mind.

Uta grew quite earnest. 'I think I can persuade him to go, Herr Bauss.'

'Excellent. Good lass. Then off you go.'

In the corridor some well-executed crayon portraits of the last Landgrave, sketched by his daughter, told of a lost world.

If Uta wanted to exit this country too – whose captives toiled mainly to produce munitions for the Russians – tonight was the night.

*   *   *   *

At mid-morning, Udo dropped in at his flat.

A trail of talcum powder footprints across the bath rug and the linoleum, indicated that Greta had liberally used this luxury item.

He saw her blotchy legs as he put his head round the kitchen door. 'Hullo.'

'Hi,' came the bored riposte.

'I can only stay for ten minutes. Make some coffee.'

'Am I your slave?'

He gave her a long hard stare.

'I'm sorry. Of course I'll make some. I feel a bit down.'

Familiar territory this. If she's unhappy it's my fault. If I'm unhappy, it's also my fault.

She came to him to be consoled. He held her like an unwanted Christmas present.

'Don't be over-possessive.'

Wounded, she asked, 'Only in the sty?'

'Quite,' he confided. 'Only in the straw, when beside your favourite boar.'

They eyed one another coldly. She could be pleasant when milking you, but soon sulked if the pandering stopped.

Eckman swallowed her indifferent beverage and left.

Outside some workmen were patching the road. The tar vapour had a minerally tang to it. He inhaled and it felt therapeutic.

This Lyskirchen lass, was she unimaginative ... or brave or blind? Anyway, she had clearly had a curious effect on the Chief.

* * * *

At ten past eleven, Christoph left his flat and descended the draughty stone stairs with two books under his arm.

In the bleak ground-floor vestibule stood two padlocked bicycles, a row of numbered letter-boxes and a dusty old bench on which sat a police lass, reading a newspaper.

Uta stood up and put the newspaper back in 2A's box.

'Good morning, Christoph.'

'Oh … Good morning.'

'May we talk?'

He gave her a nervous smile.

'Where are you headed?'

'The library.'

'Come and sit down for a moment.'

She had seemed lively enough yesterday, but today possessed even more suppressed fizz or electric energy. He noted her black eye.

She swept her coat deftly under her as she sat down and offered Christoph the spot beside her.

Leaning her face into his, she spoke quietly.

'We know that you are sticking up those "Befrei Deutschland" posters.'

She watched for a reaction and sure enough, he paled.

'N-no. How do they know?' A terrible involuntary shudder ran through him and almost beggingly, he clasped her hands.

So Bauss was right.

She extracted her right hand, leaving its glove in his rigid grip and brought it up to rest on top of his shaking left mitten.

'Shhhh!' she reproved him, watching him swallow. 'Listen carefully. You will be allowed to "escape" to the West ... but you must leave tonight.'

He gave her his troubled attention. 'Is this your doing?'

She gave a cursory squeak of laughter. 'I'm a corporal, not a field marshal.'

His eyes looked at hers and detected no deceit. He trembled again and clutched her forearm. 'How?'

'A goods train departs for Bebra from the Rohrdorf sidings at eight o'clock, yes?'

'Yes.'

'Hide on it. There will be no border checks.'

'I must wrap up incredibly well or I'll freeze to death.'

'You can take a few belongings ... a rucksack say.'

He hesitated.

'It's not a trap. Trust me. Go.'

'I'm done for if I stay?'

'Definitely. Most of us would give our right arms for such a chance.' She paused. 'You will go?'

'Yes.'

'Then good luck. You go now. Leave separately.' She smiled encouragingly.

As he handed his books in at the library, this decision to let him go seemed inexplicable.

*   *   *   *

A pale grey light bathed the Lyskirchen's living-room.

Isolde was practising her violin.

There came a knock at the door, so she went to open it.

Greta stood there in her misshapen old brown coat.

'Hullo Greta.'

'Can I come in?'

'I suppose so.'

They eyed one another uncertainly for a few seconds. 'Is Christoph in?'

'No. He's popped out.'

'Oh. Well I just came to say that I've found a new boyfriend … '

'I think he more or less expected it.'

After another awkward hiatus, she came out with, 'I wanted to tell him something else too.'

Isolde looked at her calmly but a little severely, like a foreign minister receiving a treacherous ultimatum.

'I think he's under suspicion for pasting up those "Befrei Deutschland" placards.'

Isolde showed no sign of shock and Greta was annoyed with herself for being unable to return her critical gaze.

'So you *are* a police spy?'

Greta seemed briefly tongue-tied. Then, 'I didn't go out with Christoph because I was told to. He's ended up in trouble by his own stupidity.'

Isolde exhaled softly. 'Oh well, you've done what you had to.'

'Don't look at me with pity!' Greta burst out savagely. 'You, Isolde Lyskirchen, are nothing, yet you think you're so elevated.'

She felt an urge to slap Isolde in the face.

'I do not think I am always right.'

'I'm just going to look after myself.'

'Yes. I see.'

Greta slapped her across the face.

Isolde rocked slightly, but remained silent.

Greta strode to the door and jerked it open, but in marching out a belt-loop caught on the handle and swung her round to collide with said door.

She swore, viciously tore the belt-loop free, kicked the door and slammed it behind her.

Greta, a couple of weeks back, had tried to tempt Isolde to a party to be held by the local infantry regiment. 'There'll be lots of men there,' she had said, but Isolde did not wish to meet 'lots of men'.

'One is the right number,' she thought to herself, 'or perhaps in my case, none.'

She sat down and sobbed.

*   *   *   *

Lorenz Bauss's lunch had been brought to his office.

At last he was close to cornering one shadowy enemy.

After two mouthfuls of sausage and cabbage, someone knocked.

'Come in.'

Uta entered looking quietly vibrant.

'Well?'

'He'll be on it, Sir.'

'Excellent. Your task for the rest of the day is to shadow him and ensure that he does board the train. Take a couple of hours off now, then set off.'

'Sir.'

'Even assist if need be. And deal with any interfering *Vopos*. You have my personal authority.'

Dismissed, she danced off to her nook in the barrack block.

The well had not gone dry. Due to this tip-off, Bauss felt rejuvenated. He opened Isolde's file and took out a black-and-white head-and-shoulders shot of her. 'The daughter of my great diminisher. Will you pay for her infidelity … for all the cycles of hope and despair?'

Yet together with this looming vengeance, he sensed change. His encounters with Susanne had endowed him with a dream of happiness. 'My beloved, may our wrongs be righted?'

*   *   *   *

A key turned in the lock and Christoph came in.

She smiled tentatively.

'He knelt down beside her and took her hands. 'I've been stopped. The posters … '

'Yes.'

'You know?'

'Yes.'

'But they say I can escape on a goods train tonight.'

He rested his head in her lap and she stroked his hair softly. 'Come with me Issi.'

'They won't allow that. Besides, why should I run?'

'To have a future? We haven't done anything yet with our lives … except play with toys and read books.'

'That's not so bad a list. You go Christoph. It's all right. It's meant to be like this.'

'If I get away, that ought to point me out as being the culprit.'

With a trace of a sigh Isolde said, 'I'm not sure it's that simple.'

They were still for a time.

'Go and pack some things for your journey. I'll make some food for us.'

'We've a tiny drop of wine left that father made. We'll share that.'

*   *   *   *

Greta's grandmother's only light bulb had failed. As the day's last mauve sunbeams filtered through the lace curtains, she wound up, filled with oil and lit the old Carcel-lamp, then continued reading aloud to herself, as was her habit.

She heard the knock and answered the door.

Her granddaughter she saw, was restraining an almost explosive tension.

The flickering lamp made their faces and the bowls on the dresser glint darkly.

In the scullery Greta washed the ugly silver teaspoons, all leafy and French.

'Have you seen your new man?'

'We went to the ballet yesterday.'

She saw that Greta had surrendered to lust, to havoc. Indeed if she said much to her, the girl would throw a tantrum.

The caller eyed the stuffy frills and bombazine of the old woman. She herself preferred simple skirts and blouses. Greta was utilitarian because she liked it that way. Her eye fell on the ornate newel-post, whilst the scents of rose-petal sachets tinged the air.

Although her grandmother's background was of town life, a professional father and a rather prim ladies' seminary, she was quite down to earth.

They had nothing in common. Greta said, 'I'm due to see him at his flat soon. In fact I'm on my way to buy some vegetables.'

Greta's face seemed a dusky lilac. 'You've become hard, Greta. Pour the coffee, dear.'

She did not pour the coffee. 'You imagine you're some kind of soothsayer ... that your words are touched by some ambiguous genius ... '

'A hoax, you think?'

Her grandmother recalled that the Carcel lantern had been in a nearby cobalt mine once. Her son had hidden there; a deserter.

As a child, Greta had dreamt of hugging the lamp-post at the end of the street, with her legs wrapped round it.

'Can you not cry, dear?'

Greta stared at the brown and white photograph of an old family group. In faded ink along the bottom it read, 'Die Familie Stehr – 1913.' Why was she even here?

'I think I'll leave.'

Pulling her cardigan back on, her arm accidentally knocked over the antique coffee-pot and a deluge of hot coffee splashed onto her skirt and stockings whilst the remainder ran off the table edge. 'Piss and damnation!' She leapt up angrily and smashed the prized coffee-pot on the table.

'You think you know everything, when in fact you know nothing.' Seizing her coat and handbag, she left.

Outside she almost bumped into curvy Elke, a girl who

had pipped her to the post in winning a physics study bursary. Greta went to shove her into a wall, but herself slipped on the ice.

Elke stepped back, looked down at her half-kneeling enemy and smiled sweetly.

Struggling to her feet, Greta snarled, 'Habenicht rigged it for you, didn't he?' Herr Habenicht was the *Vopo Kommissar*.

There was some truth in this, but to further annoy her Elke said, 'That's right. He pretended to give me singing lessons, but after a few *solfeggi*, we just hopped into bed.'

*   *   *   *

By mid-afternoon the light started to fade as more snow clouds swept in.

Uta had packed her cylindrical dark-blue kitbag, where previously the electric fire had been hidden. Left behind in the steel wardrobe were her ice-skates – which were almost museum pieces – and a pile of books and magazines.

Might the kitbag betray her? No one went off to training camp this near to Christmas.

She set her alarm then lay down.

Three *Vopos* were beating up Stephanie. 'Leave her alone,' she scolded them.

'Either join in or piss off,' they scowled. 'Or do you want another black eye?' They laughed.

'Everyone here buys an occasional black-market item,' she repled. 'For heaven's sake, be charitable.'

Her alarm clock burred. A quarter to five.

She made a last drink in the kitchen and half an hour later, in her uniform and with her handbag and kitbag, left the grounds of the *Grenzpolizei* building, wisely not passing through the field of vision of the Police Chief's windows.

At Essbach's modest railway station, she waited under the steel-trussed overall roof to catch the five fifty-two to Hollern. Her hefty kitbag sagged on the grubby platform beside her. She clutched a half-pink and half-mauve cardboard ticket in her gloved hand.

Nearby three schoolgirls chattered, some boxes waited on a trolley and gas lamps hissed softly.

The sharp ridges of her shoulders and the distinct shadows and outlines of her face, suggested a *détente* with the world. She appeared imperturbable and alert.

The train rumbled in, its steam-encircled engine semi-opaque, the black sheen of its paint though unusually glossy.

Six passengers embarked.

Uta intended to leave at Edstedt, which was a half-way to the Rohrdorf sidings.

*   *   *   *

The clouds had dispersed leaving the snow sparkling on the ground and on the trees in the pale moonlight. Looking backwards, he glimpsed the dim lights of Essbach.

Christoph wore all his three woollies under his jacket, two pairs of mittens and three pairs of assorted socks inside his boots. His scarf was wound a half-way up his face and in his canvas rucksack were manuscripts, some of his toy wooden figures and a little food and drink including a bar of dark chocolate which Isolde had given him.

To embolden his spirits, he thought of the freer world which beckoned, of writing and of travel. He was ready though to jump into a ditch or under a hedge if anyone appeared on the scene.

To give the signal cabin a wide berth, he struck off the road where the fields ended and the wood began. The stubble of the dead sugar beet stems crunched beneath his feet, before the silvery snow grew deeper. He waded through it up to the railway, leaving a clear trail behind him. The signal gantry loomed up to his right. The shriek of an engine's whistle pierced the stillness and the familiar puffing swelled until it passed by in a crescendo.

Political oppression had not affected Isolde. Her omnipresent God was greater than any mundane circumstance.

The steel rails criss-crossed at the junction as the tracks to Hollern left the main line. The signal lamps were all lit, so Terenz ought not to venture out of his cabin again.

He turned to the right and walked alongside the Hollern branch, but stopped at the gradient marker post.

*   *   *   *

Greta sat at the table in Udo's kitchen, her face rigid. A book on electronics lay open in front of her, but she paid it no attention. The sound of the outside door opening and closing, broke the gloomy silence.

Udo called out. 'Greta?'

She sat woodenly and did not reply. He came into the

kitchen and threw his hat and mack onto a chair before throwing her an encouraging smile. 'Everything all right?'

With a degree of catatonic stiffness, she said, 'I've read this page four times and I still don't know what it says.'

He moved up to her as though with concern and placed an arm around her shoulders.

'I just feel numb.'

'Well we all have off days when we can't concentrate.'

The man who had sat behind them at the ballet, had muttered to his friend that he could see the ballet-dancers' underwear through their gauzy dresses. Was Udo like that too? Interested only in the erotic? She said, 'I just don't care any more.'

Eckman grew more shocked at this depth of depression. He expelled a deep breath. 'Let's make some fresh coffee? I have a few beans left and I shall grind them in a particular way to liven you up.

If it helps at all, I can tell you that your old boyfriend is not going to come to any harm.'

As the percolator started to bubble, he came round behind her, rested his hands on her shoulders and started to knead them.

'Your face seems rounder ... a bit pumpkin-like.' She struggled to force some animation into her tone.

'All the better for cuddling you with.' His hands slid smoothly down onto her breasts.

Suddenly she writhed violently away, leapt up, spun round and glowered at him with burning eyes.

Udo stepped back a pace, shaken by her ferocity. 'Who the hell do you think you are?'

After a caesura of frozen fury on her part, she tipped the

table over and everything crashed to the floor.

An incensed Udo seized her by the neck. He saw all his broken crockery.

'You duped me!'

'What do I care? Get out!'

She flew at him, her teeth gritted together and her face distorted. With considerable effort he grabbed her wrists and dragged her struggling, threshing, kicking form to the floor of the passageway, where he opened the door of his flat and ejected her onto the dark landing. She fell onto her knees and then in a sitting posture clutched the banisters, breathing heavily. Her coat, bag and boots landed on top of her and the flat door banged to. She looked with indifferent curiosity down the dank stair-well with its tatty varnished woodwork, peeling cream-painted walls and soulless blank doors. She staggered to her feet, put her coat on without doing up the buttons and her boots, slowly gathered up her possessions and stumbled down to street-level.

From her inside pocket she extracted the thirty Marks and in the bleak entrance to the flats, threw them down onto the dirty concrete floor.

*   *   *   *

Uta stood on the short low platform at Edstedt until the train had left.

Her eyes gradually adjusted to the darkness and the eerie scene over which a one-third moon – white and slightly fuzzy – threw her pall of nebulous light.

In the sagging wooden shelter, she extracted a second

woolly from her kitbag and put it on under her coat, then set off through the whitesward of undisturbed ankle-deep snow, her kitbag dragging down her left shoulder. She reached the lane and as she left the little collection of houses and farms in the direction of Hollern, picked up a single trail of recent and unblurred footprints made by a man's boots.

The last cottage in Edstedt had a telephone. The pole and wire confirmed this. She dropped her kitbag behind a rhododendron bush and viewed the squat abode. Here dwelt Frau Höppner who had once taught mathematics at the High School.

Through a window Uta glimpsed her crocheting amid her heavy black furniture, the familiar wood-burning stove and an Austrian cuckoo clock.

She knocked and showed the former schoolmistress her warrant card, then asked to use the telephone on police business. She took her boots off and was shown the required instrument on an ancient sideboard. The switchboard connected her to *Grenzpolizei* Headquarters.

'Corporal Dietl here. Connect me to Herr Bauss, please. He's expecting this call.' She handed Frau Höppner a brass fifty Pfennig coin as payment. It read 'Deutschland 50 Pfennig 1950' on its obverse and had a plough and a factory on its reverse. 'Uta here, Sir. "The donkey's gone to market".' He sounded pleased. She replaced the ear-piece and sighed with relief; there were no reversals of plan.

On leaving, the deep roar of a large motor car could be heard coming from the direction of Essbach. With a strong inkling as to who it might be, Uta stepped nimbly behind some spiny rest-harrow and crouched down.

With the dark-blue kitbag now slung from her right shoulder and her handbag on her left, she set off again, into the bitter, though windless, cold.

Joos's heading for the area of the sidings could spell trouble.

The lane entered the s-bend, which took it up onto the bridge over the railway. Then it descended between fences and hedges, under the clear star-dotted heavens.

*   *   *   *

Twenty-six years before, Susanne would have been sixteen; innately girlish and with the erratic impulses which were part and parcel of her appeal.

When Bauss thought kindly of her, his heart brimmed with balmy bird-song, but it could never quite climb over the bitterness-free threshold.

Isolde's image – which both condemned him and refused to defer – foretold that ultimately he would react.

Deep bonds exist only with the woman you love. You cannot interpret the caprices of another. Life is more black and white than many will admit.

But Susanne's endless rejections? He had visited a friend in hospital in Munich, principally in the hope of glimpsing her. He had seen her in the lofty main corridor in her grey dress, white pinafore and folded starched hat. He had trembled and he fancied that she had too. No, it was no fancy, without doubt a tremor had seized her too.

Was it an inherent shyness or a willful vanity which made her act so? He had seen instances, where after scaring off a boy with coolness, the girl had then tried to

166

lure him back … but not so with Sussi.

The good sexual desire which is love comes from God. God may tease us about some things, but not about this.

The telephone rang. 'Uta here, Sir. "The donkey's gone to market".'

At last. One unbreachable defence breached.

Yet, he had lain with his Hagars, but never his Sarah.

*   *   *   *

Joos wanted a share of this confounded gold. Then he would retire to a villa in Bolivia. His enthusiasm for Bolivia had been first sparked by a children's picture book when a lad.

Brunhilde though had grown weary of failure and the neurotic Luise had gone crazy over some university pedant.

Yet this gold had to be here. They were not simply wasps buzzing about aimlessly in a bottle.

Von Papen had been Germany's Ambassador to Turkey during the war and in August 1943, had sought out a former Ottoman vizier, one Emin Arslan Muhsinzade, who had once supplied labourers and curriers to German firms during the construction of sections of the Berlin to Baghdad Railway.

He had been sounded out on the topic of keeping his country from joining the Allies, an operation code-named, 'Sheaf of Herbs'.

Naturally, this would require bribes.

Muhsinzade and two other crooked Ankara-based Seljuks were able to assist, but – given the shifting sands of fortune in the war – only if palms were crossed with sizeable 'incentives'. And they stipulated gold. 'None of your counterfeit Reichsmark confetti.'

To von Papen's chagrin, he faced the almost unbearable humiliation that he – a German – should be the supplicant. Yet he had to yield.

And so quarterly shipments began, supplied by Germany's ally, Romania.

The heavy black EMW 340 took the track to the quarry, ploughing through a layer of snow which flew up like swans' plumage.

The right sleeves of his shirt, pullover and torn coat hung loosely over his sling-supported right arm. He was driving with one hand.

Steering maldextrously, the front wheels left the two shallow ruts and a bank of snow caught the vehicle's front left wing and slewed it. Its rear slid sideways into a hollow of deep snow.

He struggled out from the unsunken driver's side. No amount of digging would free the car. A knife-sharp cold cut into him. His coat was partly open because of his sling and his trousers were too thin for such weather. He set off on foot for the signal-box which he wrongly assumed would have a telephone.

He plodded doggedly along, lifting his feet high with each step. His trousers below the knees though soon grew sodden and ice crystals filled his shoes and started to melt. He rounded the gargantuan black shape of the carriage and then swung to the left.

A depression running alongside the railway and overshadowed by trees, held a mere ankle's depth of snow. He stepped from one hassock of weed to another.

Then he spotted a row of recent dints in the snow, made by a man's boots. They crossed the tracks. He followed them. On the other side of the line, the chasm between the trees widened out and here lay some sidings with two rows of silent wagons.

With an effort he unsheathed his pistol from his left inside pocket and holding it awkwardly in his left hand, advanced cautiously.

CHAPTER NINE

In the Johanneskirche candles burnt on a large Christmas tree, which stood to one side of the nave. At the inner end of the pew next to it, Bauss looked at a red glass bauble and espied his own swollen face.

The congregation was tightly packed and all wore thick coats and scarves.

The Saint Lucy's Day service began with a medieval carol *Hodie Christus natus est*. Apart from the choir, a set of chiming bells accompanied the refrain, there was a trumpet in D and the organ produced deep gruff short notes from a subbass pedal stop.

Apart from Bauss there were other officials and SED men present who wished to deride such absurdly superstitious events, but found that a ghostly hand paralysed them. Its strength made it hard enough not to shed a tear at times. And as to arresting anyone here, they were powerless to move.

Father Rodig spoke of Saint Lucy of Syracuse and of her death. He spoke too of loving God and said that loving God meant obeying Him.

There were traces of an older Germany here in the East; a hint of the Middle Ages when a man's knowledge was minimal and local and yet he had the deepest faith. Self-centredness had yet to conquer restraint; logic to subjugate instinct.

Bauss thought of Susanne. His eyes moistened and this created marvellous arcs of colour from the red and white lights and the candles. He discovered that if he squinted his eyes then magical circles of golden light twinkled with tiny red and lilac facetted specks. It was an optical kaleidoscope of exquisite beauty; the heavenly alternative to physics.

He could not see her, but he knew Susanne's daughter to be the organist. Of the crib display, he could spot the robed wise men backed by palms – Melchior, Gaspar and Balthazar – and above them shone a blue Jupiter, a red Mars and a green Saturn, which had once aligned themselves to give the bright morning star.

And those perfect spirits, the *Beati immaculati*, amongst which lay the source of his love for Susanne? They would never in all eternity perish.

One Lorenz Bauss, full of truth and tranquillity, would have married Susanne Dettmann. The other, created by her stubborn refusals, was playing out an uneven and unsatisfying life.

All sang *Es ist ein' Ros' entsprungen* by Praetorius. He heard the organ more distinctly this time.

*   *   *   *

Joos tracked the row of imprints which now ran parallel to a line of Titan-like if shadowy railway wagons.

The dimples stopped with an irregular patch of disturbed snow.

He smiled perversely as he peered up at the towering grim rectangle of struts bolts and boards.

A cast plate on the wagon's frame, read 'OHE' and in smaller relief, 'Osthannoversche Eisenbahnen AG'. The East Hanover Railway Company was a West German railway company. Under its destination clip too, the transshipment label read 'Hermannsburg'. The East German well-wagon next to it had on its old makers' plate; Süd-Thüringen-Bahn.

He spoke in a measured voice. 'All right. The game's up.'

There followed an intense silence.

'Come on now. Don't be shy.'

After a further five seconds a tremulous voice said, 'I surrender. Please don't shoot.'

Slowly Lyskirchen clambered over the side of the wagon which was laden with metal drums and by stages dropped to the ground. He rose from the folded posture and stared fixedly at Joos's pistol. 'I'll tell the truth.'

Joos nodded. 'First off, who the devil are you?'

'Christoph Lyskirchen,' he quavered.

'You're good at yodelling?'

'Yodelling, Sir?'

'The way your voice oscillates in pitch?'

'That's because I'm nervous.'

Joos smiled. 'Oh, I see.'

'My bag's still in the wagon.'

'Never mind that for the moment. When does this train leave?'

'Eight o'clock.'

Joos tilted his watch. He read it by moonlight. 'An hour and a quarter to wait.'

'I came too early.'

'Obviously.'

'The curfew isn't till nine.'

'I might have let you go, but ... '

'Yes, Sir?' Lyskirchen grasped at this straw.

'Stopping an escapee lends authenticity to my real purpose here.'

The timorous boy was unsure whether to grovel or to risk a sudden attack.

'So ... it looks like it's bad luck?' He heard a soft crunch on the snow behind him and started to spin round, his breath forming a helix.

Corporal Dietl had put each foot down as quietly as possible.

He just glimpsed her as the flash left the muzzle of her pistol and a faint pinky glow momentarily lit up the nearby pine branches. The thud and the sting of the bullet hitting just to the left of his backbone and at armpit level, surged up into his head. His coat flounced outwards with the turning movement, his legs crumpled, his neck arched, his hat fell off and his good arm jerked, dropping his pistol.

The range had been less than three yards. Uta lowered her weapon and reopened her left eye.

Squirming on the ground, Joos tried to reach his pistol. His foe bent over him and a second bullet – fired through her folded hat to muffle it – struck his neck. Bandit-like she had a scarf wrapped round the lower half of her face.

She watched him until she were sure he were dead, then eased her pistol's safety catch on and reholstered it. Christoph, like a hare stunned by fear, felt his skin prickle.

And thinking of Thilo, the police lass said, 'What's good for the goose is good for the gander.'

She squatted down beside the body and extracted its identity papers and some money from its pockets.

'Who was he?' asked Christoph.

'M.f.S. – *Staatspolizei* ... Berlin.

There's the possibility that a woman called Luise might be with him, so keep your ears pricked up.'

'How did he get onto me?'

'I think it was just chance. Perhaps he saw your footprints?'

She inspected Joos's pistol. It was indeed an ungainly World War I, P08 Luger as she had thought. Her torch lit up the word 'Erfurt' engraved on its toggle. She checked it had rounds in its magazine, re-cocked it and handed it to Christoph. 'If anything happens, push this lever forwards with your thumb, aim it and pull the trigger.'

Christoph asked, 'Are you here to make sure I leave?'

'Yes, but also ... '

'Also to abscond?'

She nodded. 'Might the signalman have heard the shots?'

'It's Terenz. If he has, he won't come out. He knows all about this lot.'

She moved close up to her new ally and touched his forearm as a sign of intimacy. 'We must drag this body into the trees and cover it.' Then, staring at the face-down form, she thought, 'Thilo, now you can rest in peace.'

* * * *

Werner Stege had visited Essbach on the pretext of inspecting the factory which made the glass lenses for signal lamps, but was now on his way to The Hague to sign a contract by which East Germany would build ten medium-sized cargo vessels for a Dutch shipping line.

Both Joos and Luise had passed their findings on to him.

At Utrecht the other travellers in their compartment alighted from the train, leaving Stege and his security man alone.

'Schwarzbauer, tonight we are booked in at The American Hotel on the Leidse Plein in Amsterdam? We have no official tasks this evening. How would you feel about us each going our separate ways?'

'Well Sir, I had been wondering how to subtly suggest that myself.'

'Excellent. This is our fourth trip abroad together … I think we trust one another?'

'Quite so, Sir.'

'As long as we both make breakfast for eight o'clock tomorrow morning?'

Later, Stege walked some way from the hotel, making sure he were not being shadowed, then took a taxi to the western fringe of the city.

Beside a creek, lined with boats moored to small private landing-stages, he found the house; compact, built of pinkish bricks and with green shutters. It was fronted by gravel, white wooden palings and diminutive box trees in tubs.

A lamp-lit slate plate read, 'Johann and Lorraine.' He sighed. 'Not very promising.'

A mortise lock's bolt clunked back and a shy but pretty lass of about thirty opened the front-door.

'Good evening. I'm looking for an Ingrid Stehr? Or perhaps a Johanna von Geisberg?'

The girl called over her shoulder, 'Johann?'

The scraping of a 'cello ceased and a stocky woman in her fifties appeared.

Werner raised his hat and gave himself as, 'Herr Heinemann. From East Germany.'

'Oh. And are you looking for something?'

'Yes. For thirty-nine "somethings" actually.'

'Come in.'

The sitting-room, with its dark furniture and rosy cushions was cosy yet anaemic. There perhaps lurked too a twinge of belligerence in the air?

Lorraine, from Inverness, had dark hair and wore black tights, a red and blue tartan skirt and a navy cardigan. Physically she was quite a stunner, but life's juices had sadly ebbed away. Stege's own wife was only half as pretty, but with five times the vitality. With her he could have a most satisfying and cathartic ding-dong.

The Scottish lass sat quietly beside Johann.

Some dog-eared Russian playing cards lay on the coffee-table, also some sweets on an old ceramic plate with a family crest on it.

'You once lived in the Eastern Zone, yourself?'

'Yes. Briefly.'

'And then in Oldenburg?'

'For a time, but the gangs there made it scary ... and not just the boys.'

'The girls were worse,' appended Lorraine.

'The Dutch are generally liberal ... though lately, around the Herengracht, there have been a number of murders ... and all of them homosexuals.'

Johann wore dark pink hosiery, puffed-out indigo breeches, a mustard-coloured ruff-collared shirt and a broad gold chain, vaguely reminiscent of medieval court attire. Her cropped grey hair had been dyed pale blonde.

'Well … shall we discuss business?'

Johann stated, 'I made an offer six years ago, but you baulked at my request for twenty-five per cent.'

'I was not involved in that. An issue of trust perhaps?'

'I proposed that they deposit the money with an independent law firm here, who would only release it after the merchandise had been recovered.'

'They could have denied it, I suppose?'

'I had a contingency plan for that.'

'And … you told them where one block was?'

'Yes and sent an invoice, which they evidently threw in the bin.'

'Why was one block alone by itself?'

'Aha. That would be telling.'

'You hold the key to this substantial wealth … and yet can't touch it?'

'My offer remains. What else can I do?'

Stege adjusted his position. 'I have to tell you, that I am not a government agent and so do not have the means to make an advance payment.'

Johann and Lorraine held hands.

'Then I cannot proceed.'

If only he could coax Lorraine into bed and ask her? 'Hmm … it's tricky.'

There were four birthday cards on the dresser. One – with a picture of a cheese tart – said, 'I'ld love a quiche Lorraine,' but the 'quiche' had been crossed out and replaced with 'quickie'.

Johann saw him smile. 'She's hard to offend.'

'That means that no one has yet worked out what her ego is.'

'She doesn't have an ego.'

'Oh? Perhaps you've destroyed it.' He glanced at Lorraine. 'You could have been Tatiana from Eugene Onegin ... and a lovely one too.' His look changed to a smile. 'Spend the night with me? Surely I can please you more than this freak?'

Johann leapt up angrily and the others followed suit. She thrust out her chest, to face this challenge. 'Get out.'

'Don't be judgemental, Herr Heinemann. She's very kind.'

'I can see in her face that she isn't.'

'I said, "Get out."'

'Oh, belt up.'

An oil painting showed two naked girls with garlands draped around their erotically-posed bodies; a labyrinth of pristine flesh, backed by angels and sorcerers.

'Is this one of your synthetic fantasies?' He flicked Johann's rubber breasts. 'And these? Mini-Venusbergs?'

Johann pushed his chest.

He threw back a quite unexpected and very forceful punch.

She crashed backwards into the dresser, some glass broke and her nose gushed blood.

Werner eyed Lorraine. 'You silly, stupid girl. What a waste.'

She held her fingers to her cheeks and trembled.

'Don't scream. I won't hurt you. Tell me where it is and I promise we'll cut you in.' He gripped her forearms gently but firmly.

She shook her head. 'She's never told me.'

He swore, then picked up a bottle, broke it, rammed it into Johann's face and left.

*　　*　　*　　*

On his return from the church service, the Oberkommissar summoned the duty officer.

Bauss's heart performed strenuous acrobatics, though it was now or never. Like a condemned bondsman he saw a chance to be avenged on the harbinger of his downfall.

He formulated the charge in rhetorical legalistic language. 'For printing subversive literature ... '

He heard a knock.

'Come in. Eckman, I have a job for you.'

'Sir?'

'You were the detective lead here?'

'The Lyskirchens, Sir?'

Bauss imagined Isolde as a schoolgirl, quieter than her mother, not so daft though perhaps mildly amused at times. 'Bring in Isolde.'

'Not Christoph, Sir?'

'He will not be at home.'

Alone again, Lorenz moved unsteadily to an armchair. 'Susanne fled, leaving me bereft ... and susceptible once more to those crowding shapeless shadows. *You* have condemned me to this. She is your dark messenger, sent to mock those icicles round my battered heart.'

He ground his buff teeth, screwed up his eyes and his neck went into spasm.

*　　*　　*　　*

Greta trudged slowly back to her lonely garret.

Folk were streaming home from the Saint Lucy's Day service, but she hardened her features against their smiles and turned off down an alley veiled in fog.

It led to the bombed ruins of a granary, a dough of broken masonry topped with snow; a burnt bun with icing on it. Any spared or scorched beams had been pillaged for fire-wood long since.

A posse of loitering youths saw her and sauntered to an ambush position beside a chicane. Greta turned but they trotted briskly up behind her and seized her handbag. She struggled to claw it back but one end of the strap's stitching tore and its contents spilled out onto the icy black ground. She bent to gather up her belongings, but was pushed and stumbled onto a pile of wet broken bricks. It was dark here and silent; with no one to help her. The lead jackal took her purse. His lackeys kicked her a few times, then left.

In her attic she flopped onto the bed. The shapes in the wall-paper mutated to bugbears, to sex-craving men with lolling tongues.

She jerked her skirt down to its maximum descent. 'I can brush you off at any time,' she snarled.

The wall-paper's tedious and talentless design summed up the world's horrid doleful reality, its abundance of vile humanity; grizzly black sheep all taunting her.

She dozed off and dreamt.

She was at a party, sipping a liqueur and wearing a skirt with a long vulgar split in it.

'Is she a slapper?' Isolde asked Udo.

'Yes, but … I can't imagine that you know what a slapper is, Isolde?'

'But she's right,' commented her professor.

'Perhaps a lucky guess?'

'So Isolde, what's the difference between a tart and a slapper?'

'Well, do tarts wear short skirts … and use lots of make-up?'

'Yes.'

'They sit cross-legged on bar stools, pout and wait to be bought drinks and flattered?'

'Very good. Now what's a slapper?'

'Well, they just want to get on with it?'

In a sweat, Greta woke up.

*   *   *   *

Surprises come in two forms – good and bad – and as Goitschel was now the recipient of active affection from a leggy young woman, this – as far as he could tell – fell into the 'good' category.

Luise often pretended to be proud, but some need had now dented this façade, fought with and reduced this inclination.

She had spent the previous night in Torsten's flat and tonight she returned. She wore a black linen dress with a red waist tie and her dark hair had been tied up with a broad red band. She had also brought with her a box of groceries.

She wanted the affection of this curious recluse and so paid no heed to its seeming idiocy. Her thin but mobile high-arched brows spoke her thoughts in encrypted form.

As they sat on the sofa, munching cheese and biscuits and sipping a cloudy white wine, they had not noticed the soft screech of brakes outside and so were utterly taken aback when the main door – under the impact of a violent kick – flew open.

They were still rising from their seats when Eckman entered clutching a sub-machine-gun. He wore a military combat version of the blue *Grenzpolizei* uniform with a forage-cap and heavy boots.

Two other *Grenzos* entered the room.

Eckman's weapon went off accidentally, holing the wall in three places just below the ceiling. Whilst suppressing his surprise at this accidental discharge, he ordered, 'Grab her.'

Luise was trying to work out what was happening. 'What's going on?' she insisted with rather uncertain authority. Had her uncle suddenly been toppled in Berlin?

The two sturdy privates held her splayed arms.

Eckman cockily savoured his power. 'We are arresting you Isolde Lyskirchen for ... '

'Who?! I'm not Isolde Lys-whatever. I'm Luise Stege and an officer in the M.f.S.'

The grip on her arms relaxed noticeably. Identity cards were examined, weapons lowered and abject apologies begun. 'I'm immeasurably sorry, Miss Stege ... '

A motionless Torsten realised that they were after the girl in the opposite flat, but forbore to enlighten them.

Luise, who was trembling with a combination of shock, anger and relief, was noting down Eckman's details from his warrant card and demanding that he organise a carpenter to come round and fix the door straight away.

Eckman, unable to separate emotion from facts, appeared simply ludicrous.

*　　*　　*　　*

Christoph had dragged the corpse into a drift-filled ravine and then pushed small avalanches of snow onto it. A deer leapt over a fallen branch.

He thought of his sister … but he was committed now.

He retreated to the wagons, walking backwards and hauling a fallen branch to obscure his tracks in the ice-crusted snow.

It was comforting to have Uta with him. She was practical too; the sort to weigh things up, decide what to do, then give it her best shot.

She had walked behind the trucks towards the glimmers of light from the signal-box. From behind the wheel of a goods van, she peeked under its main frame.

Terenz sat in the signal-box reading. She watched him for a few minutes as she stood in a shallow pit with the bell-cranks and rods which changed a nearby set of points.

Back with Christoph, she gave him a hug.

Oblique rays from the naked moon caught their faces, the snow and the steel wheel rims, images which were stark and wholly black and white.

'This wagon's the best,' Christoph proposed. 'The vans are locked and those long cast-iron pipes will be like wind-tunnels.

She retrieved her kitbag, dragging it also to cover her

path. Like an Olympic shot-putter, Christoph threw it high enough to clear the wagon's side.

The temperature on such a cloudless December night could fall to minus twenty-five.

'Does this train usually leave early, on time or late?'

'It's *never* early, rarely on time and anything up to five hours late.'

'Then we have at least an hour to kill. Come.'

Their boots grated on the hidden angular lumps of ballast between the sleepers as they walked along the middle of one of the empty tracks. Near the old carriage a ray of moonlight shone on the windscreen and chrome trims of the stuck and listing EMW. With her pistol drawn, the policegirl climbed the vertical steel steps onto one of the carriage's balconies and entered its gloomy saloon. *Goneril* was not there. 'Come on,' she whispered.

Inside, Christoph took off his boots and picked off lumps of snow which were stuck to his socks.

Uta went outside again to search for signs that anyone else had recently been there.

She came back into the carriage and touched his arm. 'A breeze is springing up. If it blows the snow about it might hide our prints.'

They sat down on the upholstered though damp side-seats.

'When the train arrives from Halle, they'll uncouple the brake van, couple up those wagons and then hook the brake van onto the rear again. The fireman – as he checks that all the brakes are off – will walk the whole length of the train … on both sides.'

*　　*　　*　　*

Isolde sat alone in the flat. It was dark except for a candle burning on the kitchen table. She sipped a glass of water and read softly, 'Be happy if the day is good ... '

She stopped and listened, but heard nothing. ' ... but if it is full of tribulation, remember that God gave it too ... '

She rose and put one of the last logs into the stove. The hinged iron plate banged down with a metallic ring.

She viewed the attic ladder. Should she lift the short loose floor-board, take the remaining posters and the printing set from between the rafters and burn them? No, she would not try to outwit anyone.

She listened again. A floor-board outside the door creaked. She sat down.

The door burst open, accompanied by a splintering of the frame around the lock. Eckman, Sergeant Hartwig and Private Baumeister entered with pistols.

'Seize her!'

The two rankers moved together, collided and fell to the floor in a heap.

'Idiots!'

They disentangled themselves and stood up.

'Switch the sodding light on!'

The nervous young Baumeister went to the lamp near the piano and did so, but the bulb blew immediately leaving the luminosity as before.

Eckman had returned to the station after his first blunder, been called a 'useless turnip' by Bauss and smarting heavily, had returned chastened to Keplerstrasse.

'Who are you looking for, Herr Rittmeister?'

'Fräulein Isolde Lyskirchen.'

'I am she.'

Hartwig gripped her upper right arm with his left hand.

'Keep her there Hartmut.' Eckman started to climb the ladder.

'I can tell … '

'Quiet. We've had reports about you,' growled the Sergeant.

The mere purity of her face rebuked him. Her presence alone made his own uninnocence stand out.

In the attic Eckman found the light switch on a cross beam and turned it on. He probed the shorter floor-boards near the hatchway and located the loose one. He smiled grimly as he removed a roll of two posters – briefly verifying his find – and then discovered the child's printing set. One 'T' had a damaged serif. The 'T' in 'DEUTSCHLAND' on some posters had had this defect on its cross-stroke.

Reversing down the ladder he showed these items to his colleagues. 'You witness that I found these here?'

'Yes, Herr Rittmeister.'

'Is this pernicious literature yours?'

'No.'

'Why should I believe you?'

'Because I tell the truth.'

Hartwig struck her across the face.

Eckman pulled out one of the other dining chairs from under the table and sat on it, his legs splayed out in front of him and his torso reclining at an angle. He took her purse out of her basket which stood on a third chair and quite openly pocketed the few low-value coins and a two-Mark note. He spotted the Bible. 'Ah, a king's laity contending for the starry robes?' As she refused to be drawn, he added, 'Do you think we have already decided your fate?'

'I imagine so.'

'Did you print those posters?'

She remained silent.

'Why don't you answer me?'

Isolde shrugged slightly. 'Because you won't believe me.'

The Sergeant gave her a second forceful backhander across the mouth.

The Captain watched as some blood trickled from her cut lower lip with a modicum of satisfaction.

Eckman stood up, kicked her leg and also hit her.

'Take her away.'

His two assistants manhandled her roughly, shackling her hands behind her back and giving her no opportunity to put a coat on. They marched her out, meeting a carpenter with his tool bag as they went.

As Eckman pulled 2E's damaged door to, the carpenter knelt down to start work.

'That door there, you blundering incompetent. 2F not 2E.'

CHAPTER TEN

Greta, quick to see faults in others, vicious and depressed, passed the tannery, then drifted into the arboretum. Its boating lake and bushes were popular in summer, for courting, picnics or just taking a stroll, but on a winter's evening it was dark and deserted.

Although the moon's silver bravura glistened on the roof of the flour mill, the park lay in deep shadow.

Her scarf caught on an unseen prickly bush.

She swore, stumbled down an unseen stone step, righted herself, then clung to a yew tree. She felt the knobbly grooves of its rough bark press into her lower body.

It spoke to her. 'True gold I further refine in my furnace, to be re-used by the Master. False or impure gold, I tip into the nebulous chasm of forgetfulness.'

She wanted the watchful moon to go away. Why was it there? Science could not truly explain it.

'Help me,' she said to the tree, but it did not reply.

The first diffraction line of hydrogen, a pure single-wavelength deep red, was beautiful. Could she not be like that?

She collided with an ancient Turkish bronze cannon, *Az Zahabi*. She sat astride its snow-blotted verdigris-covered barrel, which was mounted on rough-hewn wooden baulks.

From her tan handbag, with its string-repaired strap, she took a razor, unscrewed its handle and extracted the blade.

So this was it? The end of the line? She had to get off for she could bear it no longer.

*   *   *   *

The wind had increased to force four and blown the powdery snow around enough to at least blur their tell-tale bootprints.

Using the thin rays of moonlight, Christoph opened two tins of cheese using the tiny army tin-opener on his fellow conspirator's key-chain. They ate using clasp-knives.

Standing on the balcony, with the matt black frieze of trees rustling, he heard an owl hoot and saw a strip of cloud creep across the waxing moon.

Uta appeared beside him.

'We'll board the train after the shunting's done,' he said dully, then stifling a sob, 'I'm so troubled about my sister.'

She took his arm. 'Don't feel too bad. You couldn't have saved her.'

Inside the signal cabin in the Hassbruch cutting, the light from an oil-lamp and the stove glinted attractively off the burnished brass and copper instruments.

The goods train climbed out of Essbach. The points and the signals on the gantry were set to the Hollern branch. The telegraph pinged and its disc – half-red and half-blue – rotated. When a direct current passed one way through its magnetic coil, it showed red, when the other way blue.

Six or seven minutes after leaving this block, the train would reach Rohrdorf.

Hearing the whoop of the engine's whistle, the fugitives watched from the balcony of the old carriage.

The boiler of the bituminous and carbon-encrusted engine seemed to be covered in blisters, like a skin disease. Its fire emitted a red glow and its external pipe-work leaked and hissed. Its brass works plate, bolted to its main frame read, 'Preussiche Staatsbahnen – Lokomotivfabrik Breslau 1906'.

Uta looked up. 'It's starting to snow.' The white arc of the moon had paled.

The tedious sequence of clanks and bumps took half an hour. It ended after the fireman, having lifted the three heavy links of chain onto the brake van's hook, stumped past for the last time, his head bowed into the light but diagonally-angled flurry of snow-flakes which graced this otherwise prosaic scene.

He climb back onto the engine's footplate and a shrill whistle signalled the train's readiness to leave.

The would-be stowaways headed to their chosen wagon, their feet crunching the coarse ballast under the snow. Uta placed a foot on an axle-box, gained a foothold on the lower lip of the main girder and with her left hand catching the top of the planked side, managed to straddle it and land flat on the large dark drums, before dropping into a gap between them. With Christoph aboard too, they wrestled with the unwieldy tarpaulin, pulling it tent-like over their heads.

These steel drums bore Cyrillic lettering.

A semaphore signal clanged down and its light changed to blue. With painful puffs the engine's pistons and connecting-rods made their first slow strokes, reversing the train off the Hollern branch, back onto the main line.

*   *   *   *

The clock in the cell read twenty to nine. The Police Chief sat in front of a plain desk wearing a strange look of incipient contrariness.

Before him sat a handcuffed prisoner. One side of her lower lip and her left eye were mauve and puffy.

Bauss had trapped his victim, yet felt illogically fearful.

Love, so often the deceiver, offered its fatal food of bewitchment.

He wore shirt sleeve order uniform. Eckman stood in the shadows.

'We have expended a lot of effort hunting for the printer of these incitements to disorder. So have the *Vopos*.

Like your father, you're a crusader wishing to overthrow the *status quo*?'

On finding himself ignored, he nodded to Eckman, who came forward and punched her heavily on the side of the face.

'You arrogant sow!' he uttered softly.

She refused to look at her questioner or to speak. Yet because she knew her end was near, the pain seemed merely dull, even unreal.

A train huffed and puffed faintly in the distance. Trains seemed to be the only things which moved at night, like ferries to the underworld.

The Chief of Police opened a solid silver hip-flask embossed with the old Landgrave's falcon and took a swig with an unsteady hand.

He saw himself travelling in the compartment of an old-fashioned railway carriage. Isolde's face was uninjured.

'Do you know our destination, Lorenz?'

'No.'

'These carriages are blue, green, red ... '

'Shall I end up in a different one to you?'

'Perhaps not.'

The train began to slow. Bauss stood up. He came back to reality and aghast, realised that she was dead.

*   *   *   *

Greta wriggled out of her coat. Its label read 'Ehelolf and Barth' inside the collar, an old military tailors in Berlin. Its heavy neat's-leather had been worn, scuffed and stretched through long usage, starting with her aunt, who had commanded a barrage balloon company in the Ruhr.

She pulled up the left sleeves of her cardigan and blouse and with a wooden intensity, took the blade and cut firmly into the crease of her left elbow, a little inside of centre. It opened a large soft vein, but then hit the brachial artery and her sticky invisible blood pulsed out.

She had once been pretty in a comely, bucolic sort of way, but unaware of her homely, rose-cheeked appeal, had pursued the more highly-esteemed sensuality of the stylish or the titillatory.

Martin Nagel had ogled her at a Party conference eight years before, before boldly encircling her with his arm. She had stiffened but not disengaged. He was fifteen years her senior.

Carousing with her, a hand idly gravitating towards her right nipple, her coy maidenly reactions had pleased him. Her own teenage hormone levels too had begun then to demand more than just marching under a swathe of red banners.

Her hands rested on her cold leather handbag. She closed her eyes.

The artery had clotted off but not the vein.

Odd shapes swam across her field of vision, flickering flames atoning for the cold yet heralding a terrifying and carnal darkness.

*   *   *   *

Her head hung down and her shoulders sagged like a rag-doll's.

Eckman felt her wrist. 'No pulse, Sir.'

Her patched skirt and her shabby grey blouse did not detract from her inert perfection; drab clothes adorning a quiet dawn.

Everyday clothes of that era were invariably of a single colour.

'We've missed the boat.'

'We have evidence, Sir. No need for a confession.'

'She's tricked us … escaped.'

Udo seemed puzzled.

'Like Judith … or Deborah.' Bauss waved at the cell door. 'Leave.'

Eckman and Hartwig left.

An arcane lassitude sealed his lips. Like a sex offender, after the frenzy of the deed, he is sober and ashamed and horrified by what he has done.

'Sussi, your lack of love is the horseshoe nail without which my realm is doomed.'

Being a virgin, she had been undeveloped yet subtly radiant, authentic and unspotted.

Bauss put his head into his gnarled hands. His secret melancholy made him periodically or cyclically perverse, but why?

'Is anyone wicked without reason?'

*   *   *   *

Shock-waves bounced and ricocheted down the line of trucks – a domino effect – but they were off.

A cross-wind blew the cinders and smoke to one side, but the tarpaulin misbehaved. It was minus eighteen and snow clung to their hair, collars and coats.

Christoph had three woollies and a padded jacket, Uta two woollies and her sturdy uniform coat.

At Sättelsrode a deep Pratt-truss girder bridge crossed a tributary of the River Werra.

'How long will this take?' she shouted.

The engine's whistle shrieked.

'To the border … two hours?' Christoph lifted the edge of the bowlined and toggled tarpaulin. Grey-white meadows and icing-sugar-covered farmsteads jolted slowly by. 'After Eisenach, it'll swing south.'

Uta spoke into his ear. 'Supposedly I have a cousin in Austria. And you?'

'There was a Birgitte in Stamboul, but … '

'Become a playwright then?' She smiled into the darkness.

'That Terenz … what a gossip?'

On they rolled, rocking to and fro, growing ever colder

and trusting that this crazy escapade might lead to a new life … and perhaps some happiness.

*   *   *   *

With the door repaired, Torsten and Luise went to bed.

The hour of curfew – or 'couvre feu' or 'cover the fire' as he explained – had long since passed.

At thirty, Luise longed to settle down.

They faced each other under the covers. 'When you appeared yesterday, I thought I'd lost my job. I expected to be told to report to an engine shed as a cleaner … or something similar.'

She stroked his hair.

'The strange thing is that I wouldn't have minded.'

'My omnicognisant' – that was her nickname for him – 'if you had cleaned engines, you would have done it well.' She nuzzled into his chest like a mole trying to burrow into hard clay.

'That commotion earlier … '

'I think it was just a mistake.'

'I suspect they wanted the girl who lives opposite.'

'What's she done?'

'I don't know.'

They were serious for a time.

'No one here can feel wholly at ease … not even the high-ups.'

'Least of all the high-ups.'

'My sweet, this secret purpose of yours … Socrates remarked on women having the privilege of seclusion … '

'That was a different society. Today we have to be active

… out and about.'

'I spent time in Greece in the war … in the Peloponnese. The mountains and the wild flowers made a deep impression.' He remembered the opal-green sea and a tortuous tree near a dusty village. 'My Spartan maiden? Would you dance beside the Eurotas in the moonlight?'

In early Greece, he had read, in Arcadia – that mountainous area of the Peloponnese anciently known as Drymodes, due to its oak trees – the sequestered and acorn-eating inhabitants were either solitary shepherds, adept warriors or pastoral musicians. Their speech preserved traits of historic dialects and they believed themselves older than the moon.

The wine of Arcadia, when kept in a goat's skin and near to a fire, would become cloudy and chalky and this when drunk supposedly gave wisdom and visions.

As they made love, she wondered if he were the gold she had come in search of? She felt so calm, so content.

Luise had goaded Thilo into selling tins of cheese on the black market at a mere twelve Pfennigs a time, but had not realised that Joos meant to kill him.

*   *   *   *

Brunhilde had been to Malabar Terrasse – or *Afrika* as they had code-named it – and found neither Joos nor Luise.

From the exchange she rang the hospital, the Hotel Lindeneck and the *Volkspolizei*, all without result.

She rang her parents' home in Berlin.

'Pappa? Hello. I'm in the telephone exchange in Essbach. Both Joos and Luise seem to have disappeared?

Yesterday, in a punch-up, he had his arm dislocated, but now he's vanished ... and Luise too.'

'Hmm ... Put me through to the *Volkspolizei*. They can put their boots on and do something useful for once.'

'All right.'

'They won't be getting any leave this side of Christmas.'

'Do you mean this Christmas?'

He laughed. '*Ma belle endormie*.'

*   *   *   *

Bauss inspected the drained ivory face, this scion, branch and flower of she who had tormented him.

Darkness re-invaded him.

In the morning the larks would sing and she would not be lying in a cell with a beaten body. Her demise had been too quick.

He had wanted the wrongful trespass of physical mastery over her, but it had been denied. Yet ... the night had been evil so far, so why stop now? Heidi lived across the railway, behind the gas works. He could walk there.

He washed and spruced himself up.

The night air felt sharp and wild. Her street was damp and dark and shiny, as if tiny diamonds sparkled in a scene brushed with tar. It was cold and creepy ... and sexually stirring.

She opened the door of her ground-floor flat and seemed taller than he had remembered. Her smooth pale face glimmered, like a lantern in a mine.

In her dimly lit and cramped sitting-room, he threw off his cap and coat and tugged at his boots whilst she rekindled the stove. She seemed possessed of a strange deliberation. He wondered who was the stalker and who the prey?

He complimented her on her physical shape, but she deprecated this earnest though lust-tinged admiration. They sat beside one another, she awaiting his advances.

Her hypnotic energy drew his baggy and rough anatomy forwards. It coiled itself around her firm slender form. They kissed and fondled, her stimulus more overtly sensual than Céline's.

Black coffee and cake appeared; a priestess handing the symbolic food of life to an initiate; a rite in a dark temple.

'You look fit enough tonight?'

'Yes ... though I've a cataract, a nasal polyp and hard skin on my feet ... '

'Oh ... a sinking ship then? Full of holes?'

'I had a bad tooth out last week, so one less hole.'

'Or one more?'

'True. An oxymoron.'

She lent him a pair of old ski-ing breeches in lieu of pyjamas. He displayed his collection of pointed ochre teeth as they toppled into bed.

An orange-spotted spider lurked under the lamp-shade.

Heidi knew he was not happy.

'Put your nurse's uniform on.'

She did so and they had sex.

Their contrived smiles ceased as they were subsumed by this event.

'Slowly.' She held him. 'Leave it in.'

A trail of woeful sparks floated through the forest of his mind. He sensed no emotion, no rapture, only the physical pinnacle.

She grabbed his blunt stick a second time, the sentry rigid at his post. His cherished phantoms, like mirages, collapsed in this loveless desert. On top of her, he imagined she were Isolde, then Célines, then Uta.

She thought of her worn-out father driving hogs to market and peeling rushes for rush-lights. He had said to her, 'Just use the bastards as much as you can.'

'It's Saturday tomorrow,' she said. 'I only have to work till midday. We'll have another coffee … then do it again.'

CHAPTER ELEVEN

The sloping boulder beside the railway – the one near to the signal post to which Uta had clung – had been in pre-historic times an altar, around which girls stabbed their breasts with bone needles and without pain because of their frenzy or ecstasy.

Incantations, the full moon, the chase of the deer and the offering to the priestess all conspired. She had worn a cherry-coloured dress down to her knees and on top of it a shorter orange tunic. Again on top of this a belted brown leather cuirass with a shallow gold disc over each breast, each etched with runes. On her legs were leggings, wound round with leather thongs.

And I too may still conjure simple forms of magic, such as when Joos skidded and dislocated his shoulder.

So a grim and turbulent day has passed in Essbach, but our surviving actors and actresses are starting to see how the chaos will settle into order; how their shortcomings will be ingeniously resolved.

*   *   *   *

In Thuringia the weight of the snow had made every twig dip, but farther West the weather had been less severe. The three-eighths moon lay on her back.

Uta sat on the floor of the wagon and shuddered, whilst Christoph held one edge of the tarpaulin aloft and peered out. The parallel rails reflected the moonlight, as did the snow-capped arboreal landscape.

Could he envisage angels descending on this wintry night?

They had eaten the precious bar of dark chocolate which Niehaus had given to Isolde, but they longed for a hot drink.

Suddenly the junction at Förthastädt was upon them. The train slewed to the right and crossed a long girder bridge which spanned the meandering River Werra. Beneath the black sharp-edged steelwork, flecks of foam in the rock-dotted water could be glimpsed.

'This is it – Gerstungen – the crossing point.'

He could make out the sidings and concrete buildings where trains were inspected and searched. On a signal gantry ahead, seen in a faint blue luminescence, were the black skeletons of semaphore arms. All their lights showed red.

With a final screech of the engine's brake shoes, they lurched to a halt.

Uta struggled to her feet and straightened out her coat.

The pair peered out at the hazy orange arc lamps some way ahead and a board reading 'Grenztruppen der DDR'.

A violent jerk backwards made them fall over.

'That's the engine uncoupling. Probably hours now to check the paper-work.'

They breathed shallowly and listened. There were odd shouts in the distance, but no soldiers or border guards appeared.

A second engine jarred the line of trucks, then suddenly, wonderfully they were swaying over points and pitching from side to side as they left a loop and glided through Gerstungen station with its darkened buildings. The trucks bumped and tugged one another as the couplings became alternately slack and taut.

The old line to Heringen peeled off to the South, weed covered and blocked physically by some missing rails.

Some wooden buildings passed, then large red-on-white warning signs; 'Halt!', 'Staatsgrenze' and 'Passieren verboten!'

A massive concrete bunker drifted by, a gaunt watch-tower and swathes of black barbed wire. Tall weeds poked up between the rails alongside as would never have been allowed in Prussian days.

The orangy-grey lights of the border post grew dimmer as the train surged ahead, gaining speed, into a saucer-like, flatter landscape.

Uta hugged Christoph.

*　　*　　*　　*

Eight *Vopos* with lamps and wearing winter combat gear arrived at Rohrdorf quarry in a lorry and a light blizzard. Wotan, a huge Alsatian, sniffed the driver's seat of the snow-bound car.

'Wonderful. Nothing nicer at ten past midnight,' said the sergeant.

The dog set off, tugging his handler through the knee-deep snow. Along the railway line it went, then across it, then into the trees, to a heap of recently disturbed snow. Men with shovels quickly found the body.

The signalman was interviewed roughly. Terenz said he knew nothing. He had heard the two shots, but kept mum.

He was thrust back against the rack of tools and oilcans. He related the events of thirty hours before. They vaguely knew of this *Grenzo* police lass, Uta Dietl.

They thought to take him to the *Volkspolizei* barracks, but he pointed to his levers and telegraphs. 'And what about train movements?'

Shortly after this, a *Vopo* officer drew up at the *Grenzpolizei* headquarters, where Eckman was the duty officer. Uta's room seemed suspiciously empty. They stared at one another.

Others in the block, roused from sleep, said that she often spent a night with an aunt on a farm, but no one knew where it was.

Next they searched for Bauss. He did not answer his telephone. *Vopos* went to his flat and forced the door, but without result.

The local *Volkspolizei* Head of Division – Uwe Habenicht – was in his office, directing this circus with vigour. Finance Minister Axt wanted results.

*   *   *   *

Bauss put his arms around a stuporose Heidi who had her back to him.

The clock pinged three.

Why had Susanne not simply said, 'Yes,' twenty-six years ago? To be in each other's arms had seemed the most natural and most perfect thing in the world.

And still he hoped.

He would have preferred to be a road-sweeper, living on bread and cheese in a tiny flat with Susanne. 'What are you thinking, Sussi? You must surely regret your obstinacy?'

He thought of Isolde. What had he done? A strange silence gripped him, infinite, emotionless and spreading far out into the universe.

He had been brave, but never it seemed brave enough. Absolute faith alone could overcome; ninety-five per cent was not enough.

He was mere brush-work on the scene of life. He would soon cease to exist, be perhaps no more than a faint memory in the mind of God.

The alarm buzzed at a quarter to six. Heidi had to get up for work. She indicated the door. As he dressed, she said sourly, 'Twenty Marks.'

'Go stuff yourself.'

She was taken aback. 'What? Then what *do* I get?'

'I'll wring your brazen neck if you like?' He left and slammed the door.

Day had not yet broken out in the narrow street. The shadows were deep but not impenetrable. He saw the red glow hovering above the retorts at the gas works and heard the clang as hoppers of coal were discharged into their tops.

He walked slowly. By a half past six a few black branches from trees could be seen crossing the curtain-filtered glimmers of lit windows. It was bitterly cold, yet oddly he did not notice it.

He would seek out Susanne, up on the Baltic coast.

In Keplerstrasse, he went up to flat 2E, like a boy trespassing in a neighbour's orchard. No one had secured the door. He heard someone. A thief? He entered and saw Lieutenant Niehaus sifting through some papers. Both were surprised.

'Good morning, Sir.'

'Jörg? A bitter morning, eh?'

'Indeed, Sir.'

'I was out for an early morning walk and ... '

'I'm looking for clues ... whether anyone else was involved with the posters?'

Niehaus's collected papers were in fact pieces of music which Isolde herself had written.

The Police Chief examined a largish water-colour painting of the *Scharnhorst*. It was decidedly amateur – even childish – and showed the battlecruiser, bows on, anchored in a Norwegian fjord. A few wooden houses stood on the shore, huddled round a small white church. In the bottom corner he made out the start of the signature; 'S. Lyskirchen', before it degenerated into a squiggle. The warship with her destroyers had sought a British convoy in the Arctic Ocean under a wintry star in 1943. Into a northerly gale she had sailed only to be sunk off North Cape. A mere handful of her crew of two thousand had been picked up.

A second picture of a small boy fishing amid some reeds by a stream, was again bold though inept.

He parcelled up the first.

'Well Jörg, it doesn't need two of us to search. I'll leave you to it.'

The stove was cold and so was Niehaus. He made coffee and took in Isolde's surroundings. A few clothes, a few pencils and books, circumstances which debarred travel, forbad excitement ... none of which had troubled her.

Isolde had gone. It is surprising how quickly people forget the dead, but he would remember her.

He had discovered some of her compositions; a *sonatina* for two violins, a *preludio e capriccio* for organ and parts of a score for a ballet titled *Cristina di Bolsena*.

* * * *

The goods train rolled ponderously through farmland, round a curve on an embankment, crossed a country road then slowed. A red light glowed up ahead and a cluster of dwellings appeared. They clunked past a loop and almost stopped.

The escapees clambered over the side, straddling the thick wooden planks. Uta stood first on a buffer then down onto a brake bar before jumping off and rolling over in the line-side vegetation. They retrieved rucksack and kit-bag.

The signal lamp changed to blue and the train gathered speed.

It was two-thirty.

The small town of Lispenhaugen fortunately had a police station.

Frozen to the core they were shown by a tight-lipped constable, into a bare waiting-room with an electric fire. Uta knelt down so closely to it, that she scorched one of her mittens.

Slowly they thawed out. Uta wiggled her toes inside her thick stockings.

They slept on the benches until six, when Uta was led into Oberpolizeimeister Krauss. In his office a log fire burnt in an old grate.

She carried her two bags and her wet coat and boots and was waved coolly to a metal-framed chair.

Krauss's uniform consisted of fawn trousers, green tie and woolly and a mustardy-khaki shirt.

'Refugees seldom appear here.' He disliked paperwork and did not feel well-disposed. 'So? What's your story?'

She handed him her pistol, some spare rounds and her warrant card.

Having noted these, Krauss leant back and eyed her sceptically. Was she a policewoman? Was she not a little too mercurial, too poised? Spies on secret missions were frequently insinuated into the West, disguised as refugees.

Though Uta's eyes were bleary and her body tired, she tried to combat his suspicions. 'I am or was a *Grenzpolizei* corporal, Herr Wachtmeister.'

He smiled slightly at the title *'Wachtmeister'*. In the Federal Republic he was a *Polizeimeister*. *Wachtmeister* sounded like *watchman*. It had an almost medieval ring to it.

She handed over Joos's papers which cited the two East German ministers, Stege and Axt. Silver foil or gold? Gems or paste? And who was this Christoph? No one of any importance it seemed ... but decoration, backdrop?

She thought of her hat with the bullet hole in it, but that could be seen as a theatrical prop.

'I want no more than to be a salesgirl or a cleaner.'

He smiled ambiguously, led her back to the waiting-room, then brought her a large cup of chicken broth and a roll. 'Breakfast.'

'Thank you.'

'What are you doing with that coat?'

Uta with a pair of nail scissors from her handbag, was snipping away at the stitches which held the felt

'Grenzpolizei' arcs at the top of its sleeves. 'It is the only coat I have, Herr Wachtmeister, so I'm removing its insignia.'

Later Krauss questioned her about Bauss and Habenicht. Her answers did not seem cautious or rehearsed. The soup and the fire were slowly restoring her.

'I simply want to settle down to an ordinary, quiet life.'

He nodded.

Her truncheon intrigued him.

He collected German police force artefacts. The hand-cuffs were nothing, but the truncheon was beech, three centimetres in diameter, black lacquered and with calligraphic red Gothic script spiralling down it.

'It's a fluke that I have it. It just happened to be in the stores when I was kitted out.'

'Dated 1863,' he mused. 'From Greifswald in Prussia and for use by a special constable?

Fräulein, may I buy this? I take it you need some money? Twenty Marks?'

She accepted. 'Are we refugees held in a camp to start with?'

'Unless you have a relative here who will take you in, yes.'

'I've a cousin in the Tirol who owns a guest-house.'

'Name?'

'Emil Seitz ... in a village just to the west of Innsbruck.' Her brass police whistle on a long cord, was also verging on the antique.

Later, he helped her fill in two forms. 'You're a waitress and kitchen assistant.' He smiled. 'We have to photograph you et cetera here and when you arrive in Innsbruck you have to register with the Austrian police.'

She nodded with silent relief.

'There is no "refugee allowance" if you are going directly to another country, but the money for the whistle and the truncheon will cover a train ticket to Innsbruck.' She had too the folded notes behind her handbag's lining.

As she left, she glanced up at the green 'Polizei' sign, before climbing the icy incline and passing a bank and a chemist's on her way to the railway station.

Adverts adorning a bus shelter and the lettering on a parked lorry were brightly coloured. Even the police here moved with moderate energy. This was indeed another world.

*   *   *   *

In the East a thin golden chasm appeared, as if liquid metal were being poured into a crevice between the low stratified dark clouds. A cock crowed from a nearby smallholding.

Lorenz walked past a carpenter's workshop, where a radio played an Italian air.

A soft fuzzy orange hemi-circle nudged itself up above the misty horizon, to shine through some bare saplings.

He had drifted to the edge of Essbach. Turning back, he sought his own flat and was both dumbfounded yet strangely unsurprised to find its main door had been forced. He climbed the stairs. His dog Nero had gone.

He tugged the net curtain to one side and peered out at the patchy ash-grey shadows which edged with orange, suffused the town.

He unwrapped his new picture, painted boldly and without heed to any artistic flaws. That folly was the wonder of her.

Time now for him to be mad.

This day his life would change. His everyday work, his sitting behind his desk, had gone into history. He rewrapped the picture.

Strangely he felt little guilt over Isolde, as it were a mere catalyst to his making this necessary last step.

He made coffee. He ate his last bread roll with jam. He changed into his everyday clothes and stuffed a few biscuits and woollies into an ex-army holdall.

This task, this pilgrimage, avoided for too long, required a devout, an adoring faith.

With the holdall and a large flat package, he set off, choosing the quieter Creuzburgstrasse to reach the railway station.

He showed his pass for unrestricted travel and bought a ticket to Berlin. He would buy tickets separately at each stage of his journey, to hide his tracks.

Knowledge to older men means a fascination with the unique and the anomalous; not idle generalisations.

His train drew in.

*　　*　　*　　*

A haze-filtered morning light diffused itself through the second-storey windows of a spacious office just off Berlin's Alexanderplatz.

Four days ago Balthasar Axt had bumped into the President, who claimed to have mislaid his Finance Minister's conference speech. A pleasant surprise this, as Axt was unaware that he had even written it.

The telephone rang. 'Axt, where's this script? I'm having

no comedian on my platform without first probing his intentions.' This was of course, the original point.

Axt hated giving speeches.

Bright people have a degree of openness about their opinions, even a touch of scepticism. Only idiots are completely sure of themselves and see everything in black and white.

Besides, apart from family and friends, did anyone really care much about anyone else? Fools and oddities were of mild interest, but most people were just dull.

Behind his broad mahogany desk, Balthasar sat in a carved well-padded chair. Various flags and portraits adorned the walls. He flipped open a pad of paper, then hesitated. If they had found the gold and fled, this fatuous flannel would not be required.

The telephone jingled. Uwe Habenicht, the head of the *Volkspolizei* in Essbach told how they had discovered Joos's body at the quarry, crudely buried in a snow-drift.

'Killed? How?'

'Shot once in the back and once in the neck.'

Axt's tone became graver. 'Who did it?'

'We have no clues so far.'

'And Luise Stege?'

'No news there either, Herr Minister.'

'My daughter's at the Gasthaus Lindeneck. Make sure she's safe.'

'We already have someone there, Sir,' came the slightly obsequious reply. Did Habenicht's hand shake? It was reassuring that someone still feared him.

'Hmm. Joos had a fight, I hear and his arm was dislocated?'

'Yes. A policewoman did it.'

'What?'

'*Grenzpolizei* Sir, not *Volkspolizei*.'

'Hell's teeth,' he sighed. 'Have you found any odd items whilst searching ... er ... '

'*Odd* items, Herr Minister?'

'Yes ... er ... blocks, heavy ones ... the size of a brick cut horizontally in half ... and painted black?'

'I'll tell my officers to keep an eye open.'

Axt rang off. Had Joos and Luise been caught hot on the scent by some rival treasure-seekers?

His secretary knocked and entered with a tray of coffee jugs, a cup and a plate of crumpets.

'Minister, I took an international call before you arrived, from someone in Göttingen. They wished to speak to you personally.'

Axt played dumb. 'Göttingen? It sounds like a mistake.'

'Yes, Minister.' She retired, exiting through the ornate rococo-style doors of this former first-class hotel.

Why had this inept bank rung him here? Joos should have set up their accounts in Switzerland or Luxembourg instead of just across the border. Their instructions though had been clear; 'No contact in any form.' Yet was it the bank? Might it be someone who had stolen stuff from Joos?

Such calls to his secretary were liable to be tapped.

He swigged some strong coffee and bit into a crumpet.

The pro-German wartime Romanian government's last quarterly shipment to the three Turkish pashas had been collected from the Romanian National Bank in August 1944, just as the Red Army was sweeping down through the North of the country and collapse was imminent. Stehr, the officer in charge of the *Wehrmacht* detachment sent to transport it, had evidently conspired with the Bank's governor to steal a further eighty ingots.

The governor had escaped, but resurfaced in 1948 and bought a sumptuous villa in Crete. He then mysteriously disappeared. The grounds of his villa had been dug up by persons unknown.

Axt now saw Joos for the hot-head he was. Good detectives are not so.

The telephone rang. His secretary said, 'An international call, Sir.' She connected him.

'Axt here.'

'Herr Balthasar Axt?'

'Yes! Who is this?'

'Never mind. The State Prosecutor in Lower Saxony has frozen account number NS 112915 and ... '

'Who the hell are you?'

The line went dead.

*   *   *   *

Susanne was so weak and pale that the usually reluctant *Volksmarine* base doctor at Pütnitz had given her sick leave.

She lay in the People's Sanatorium. The ward-maid, wearing a shapeless dress and a loose puffy cap with an elastic band in its rim, brought the lunch trolley into the long ward. Usually Susanne liked the fish-balls made with mashed up fish, flour, milk and salt and served with cabbage, potatoes and white sauce, but not today.

Pütnitz was a village near a stretch of sand dunes on

the Baltic coast, with a gently sloping beach and a ruined concrete flak battery out in the water on which gulls nested. It had been a seaplane base in the thirties.

Lorenz still thought of her. That she knew. She had though, for reasons not wholly clear to herself, chosen another. And you had to live with your decisions.

She had sewn flags here for auxiliary naval vessels. They were blue with horizontal black and red stripes. The harbour for the inshore minesweepers was at Stralsund.

In the roof space above the ward she heard the scuttle of a rat. The fish-balls reminded her of a cod she had once landed. In the bottom of the boat it had spewed up a worm, a small spider-crab, a tiny octopus and a tiddler. She coughed on and off.

In a half-sleep, her days at Freiburg engine shed passed before her, cleaning and repairing damaged lamps. It had been a grimy job, but she had not minded it. She saw now the metal lanterns with their slots and brackets, the filthy sooty burners with their wicks and reservoirs and the thick plano-convex lenses for colouring and focusing the light. The brightness of the flame depended upon the incandescent particles of carbon from the decomposing paraffin oil and so they had to produce sooty flames to work well.

As she was not eating, a nurse came and gave her a glass of sugared julep.

Due to the bombing, Christoph had gone to join his father and Isolde been sent to a farm in a village in the East. With a water-colour paint-box she had spent time painting; a path through a wood, some engine lamps and a soldering-iron on a bench, herself as a student nurse –

you could not tell that it was she – and one based on a newspaper photograph of the battlecruiser *Scharnhorst*.

After the shooting of her husband, Lorenz had asked her to live with him, but she had refused and obtained a permit to move to the home of her old Uncle Gerhold on the Baltic coast, so shaking off her strange and tenacious lover.

In this, she had chosen to leave her children and live out her last years in loneliness, the last part of a life-long penalty for a perverse folly committed a quarter of a century before.

*   *   *   *

Luise and Torsten were awake, his arms coiled loosely around her.

'On Saturdays university lecturers can usually avoid work.'

She disengaged herself and swung her long legs round to sit on the edge of the bed. 'Rekindle the stove whilst I make the breakfast.'

From the kitchen corner, half-shielded by a faded wood and canvas screen, she bore crockery and knives and cheeses and jams to the table. 'Where are the bread and the milk?'

'We've run out of milk. There's one roll which is old and sad and needs eating up.'

She smiled. 'Do you need eating up too then?'

She put on her outdoor clothes and went to the grocer's across the square. With the stove burning briskly and the coffee bubbling, they sat down to breakfast.

Then they heard knocks on doors, but gentle ones.

These *Vopos* were solicitous. They sought a Fräulein Stege who had been seen in the square.

The middle-aged bachelor informed them that she was there.

Could they see her to confirm that all was well?

'My zoo contains only one creature, but a very pretty one.'

A plate hung on the wall showed, almost as children, a knightly, golden Tristan and a sweet ingenuous Isolde.

He thought of his neighbour. No Tristan had called there. Only a wicked King Mark.

*   *   *   *

Niehaus had walked home, but this Saturday morning seemed unusually quiet, almost hushed. Even the passing tram ran smoothly and without its usual grinding and squealing.

In his flat, he inspected Isolde's violin.

The outline plot for *Cristina di Bolsena* had been written out in her neat hand; the cast, scenes, dances and interludes, with stage business noted in brackets. The short overture began in C minor and ended in F major.

The opening dance in B major, moved between triple and duple time and in one section used the double-harmonic minor scale.

He would try to play it later. Like a stream gurgling over rocks, its substance would be eternal; indifferent to any audience.

*   *   *   *

Axt travelled by train in a reserved compartment.

His aide opened a bag of buns and a vacuum flask of coffee.

'By the way, Herr Minister, I passed my exam in stage two political theory.'

Axt smiled wryly for this lad had not a clue about the realities of politics. 'Who's a clever boy then?'

Farms and barns, wayside halts and hamlets rolled by. The ham rolls though were good and the coffee hot.

'Habenicht phoned again just before we left, Sir. The policewoman who dislocated Joos's shoulder, herself sustained a black eye in the fracas.'

'I've never heard the like of it. Was he trying to rape her or what?'

'Oh and Fräulein Stege has been found and she's safe and sound.'

'That's good.'

'And a girl with the maiden name of "Stehr", has been found dead in a park this morning.'

Axt knitted his brows. 'How was *she* killed?'

'Suicide, they think.'

In a heavy gun tractor, well armed with special permits and machine guns, Colonel Erwin Stehr and his squad of six had driven to the Turkish border with the three-monthly ransom for von Papen's governmental collaborators there. Returning through a lawless and partisan-infested Bulgaria – just days before it switched sides to join the Allies – they were supposedly headed to Liegnitz, but without orders, ended up in Essbach, Stehr's home town.

Everywhere were the signs of collapse.

In Wagner's *Parsifal*, the faithfulness and self-sacrifice

of the knights breaks the spell of the sorcerer. In Germany in 1944 most were either sorcerers or craven or a mix of the two.

At the quarry. Stehr had given his men a crate of brandy and later – when all were sozzled – killed five of them. One – though injured – had escaped. Stehr had hidden in an old cobalt mine, but been spotted and shot … prematurely it transpired as no one knew where he had concealed his half of the missing eighty ingots.

Two of the wooden boxes in the mine, led to its being searched. Wooden pit props bend before they break whereas steel ones give no warning. Miners had cited the danger. Galleries had collapsed and the effort had been abandoned. The surviving guard had stated that the bars had been coated with bitumen, for fear of ambush by bandits in Bulgaria.

Axt took out a book on Venice.

'Venice, Sir?'

'I went there briefly during the war. Such a fascinating city.'

'I'ld like to visit Moscow,' said Bussmann with youthful enthusiasm.

'Oh?'

'I read in Pushkin … how there he met with enlightened Muses, the hand of friendship and a maiden's touch …'

Axt cocked an eyebrow. 'Hmm … I would prepare for a disappointment, if I were you.'

*   *   *   *

Lorenz too was on a train. He had crossed Berlin on foot and caught the 4.05 p.m. to Stralsund. Its whistle shrieked as it approached a level-crossing on the flat North German Plain.

A low orange sun, the harbinger of a sharp winter evening caught the hawthorn twigs, glistening with opaque globules of frost and beside the track tufts of rime-blue grass, iced with a layer of frozen moisture. Some trees too, prism-like, diffracted the light into splinter-sharp rays. The loveliness of this pristine rural landscape captivated him.

Gisèle Bouvier, a liberal socialist who ruthlessly caricatured the East German leadership in the French press, had been lured to a conference in Leipzig, set up and later executed.

Struggling with English and Russian, the dialogue had become a 'dire-log'. Their views on how socialism should magnetise people were 'polarised' and when frozen out, someone asked if she felt 'ice-o-lated'.

On a tour of a laboratory where Rosa Luxemburg had worked briefly, Ekkehard Lyskirchen had been delegated to welcome her. This anarchist – something of a saturnine Gallic Jezebel – had worn a tight brown skirt and a rose silk blouse.

She had made her name with a 'controversial' book; that is one which assumes that everyone else is an unthinking half-wit.

Two micro-dots were 'discovered' on a security pass, which supposedly linked her and Lyskirchen to a spy ring.

This demagogue with her heavily-lidded eyes duly bit the dust together with Sussi's bogus husband.

He felt extraordinarily detached now from all this.

He guessed too that Susanne had not confided the stories of his wooing her in Munich in 1929, to her children. In this he was correct. The only woman you will ever properly understand is the one you love.

The leaden grey of dusk had descended. The train would not arrive in Stralsund until 10.18.

*　　*　　*　　*

The *Vopo* Police Chief – 'Bone-Crusher' Habenicht – had been malformed by his ogress-like wife, Ingi. Ingi though had now been reduced to a wreck by disseminated sclerosis and Habenicht too had softened.

He stood on the platform at Essbach with three of his senior officers. All were smartly turned out; best uniforms, buttons and boots hurriedly polished.

'What actually were these three Berliners doing here, Sir?'

'That we hope to find out.'

When the delayed express from Berlin appeared, wreathed in hissing steam, Minister Axt demanded an impromptu update in the waiting-room.

He wore the universal Trilby with a striped suit and an overcoat.

'The policewoman, Uta Dietl, has escaped to the West we believe, Minster. Her boss, Herr Bauss – head of the local *Grenzpolizei* – has vanished, though he spent the night with a nurse from the hospital.'

'So the old buck is here somewhere?'

'Quite, Minister.'

On the ancient Adler saloon's bonnet fluttered the Chief of Police's triangular pennant; black red and yellow stripes with the town's arms superimposed, a stone beacon in a notched ring.

'So, let's start at this *Grenzpolizei* château.'

Eckman, the duty officer for the evening, was just settling down to chops, cabbage, potatoes and cranberry sauce, when he heard a commotion in the foyer.

A *Vopo's* rifle, a Mauser 98K, went off by mistake and in a panic the *Grenzo* corporal on guard duty, unshouldered his sub-machine-gun.

'Which toss-head did that?' bellowed a *Vopo* major.

'S-sorry, Sir,' came a jittery reply.

A bewildered Eckman appeared.

Axt stepped forward.

In the operations room, Eckman found himself fumbling to explain why his Chief had sent Uta to the Rohrdorf sidings. Since he did not know, his confabulations proved unsatisfactory. He could only plead that Bauss had not confided in him.

A *Vopo* captain admired the new tape recorder. A ribbon ran between two reels and passed between small electromagnets. 'I've read about these. Finely ground iron oxide and cobalt are embedded in the plastic ribbon.'

In Bauss's office, explosive was necessary to crack the safe. They extracted the smoking map of the quarry and a singed file entitled *Operation Maria*.

'So he was spying on us?' concluded Axt. 'Who nicked this map?'

'I truly don't know, Minister,' Eckman implored. He vomited unexpectedly, bright green bile with some cranberries.

Axt observed, 'Like holly. Merry Christmas.'

The château's operations room became Axt's office.

Luise was ushered in courteously and he dismissed the others.

'So, where have you been, Miss Marie Celeste?'

'Well, I followed up a telephone intercept from Brunhilde and … I think I'm in love.'

Axt rolled his eyeballs. 'This search is supposed to be being run like a military operation. Never mind. How far had Edgar got?'

'He'd obtained an address for Stehr's ex-wife … in Amsterdam.'

'Yes. Your uncle's onto it. What's this run-in he's had with the *Grenzpolizei*?'

'The policegirl? She came to the carriage in the quarry.'

'Who sent her?'

'We don't know.'

He sighed. 'We should be living in palaces by now and instead … '

'Joos twice tried to seduce me … Co-operation and trust were poor, I have to say.'

The Minister stared at her.

She stared back.

Her uncle though was his ally. He smiled and tapped her lightly on the cheek. 'Sorry Luise … but try to think coherently. Who shot Edgar and what was their motive?'

'Perhaps that police lass shot him … defending herself?'

'You mean he tried to rape her?'

'I think it's quite likely.'

'But then she must have gone to Rohrdorf a second time?'

After a series of knocks, the door opened. 'The nurse, Frau Spitz, is here Minister.'

*   *   *   *

At Stralsund Bauss asked the stationmaster if he knew anyone who might give him a night's lodging for a fair price. As he had hoped, the man said that he and his wife would be happy to oblige for five Marks, including breakfast.

'I'll take a walk before turning in.'

He wandered along the waterfront and looked eastwards out over the old Orlogshavn. He saw the lights twinkling on a large Sperrbrecher-type minesweeper – really a merchantman of little value used to explode mines in front of a more valuable ship.

There were two patrol boats in too, bobbing on the water and a lighthouse whose twin beams swept by every ninety-two seconds.

A matelot appeared, walking his girlfriend home.

They chatted briefly and Bauss asked if the patrol boats carried nuclear depth charges? 'The modern world, you know?'

Waldemar laughed. 'I don't think so. If you threw one of those over the stern, it might blister your paint?'

Lorenz smiled. 'Yes, I suppose so.'

He sat on a bollard and faced the cold wind scything in from the Baltic. 'Susanne Mathilde Dettmann,' he sighed, 'shall I see you tomorrow?' A hawser, looped around his bollard, grated as the ship it held swung sideways in the basin. The cranes above the shipyard some way to his right were faintly visible in the night sky.

Black shapes were moving on the water. A tug was towing a small tanker towards a jetty. No need to visit Africa or Japan, there was enough here to last him a lifetime.

For once the way ran straight.

Next morning he took the local train to Ribnitz and there in a drizzle of sleet left the station along a path which ran alongside a disused spur to Pütnitz airfield with its ex-Luftwaffe buildings.

A gigantic hanger built in the late thirties loomed dimly in the mist, dominating the skyline.

The Russians were now using the base. As he drew closer, he could see the shoddiness of the recent GDR erections compared to the excellence and solidity of those of the Third Reich era; hovels almost, made of poor materials and with a lack of skilled workmen.

Yet today was for reciting, 'Susanne, I love you,' even more than usual. This bond was no flippant caprice, no idle infatuation, but true gold dust, sent from heaven.

His true self could only exist in loving her – she was the other half of his soul. Goblins suckled themselves on the vacuum of this thwarted love. A couple of times in Munich when he had tried to find her, her friends had been kind to him and this he knew, meant that they knew that she loved him too.

A sign pointed to the group of low buildings which comprised the sanatorium. They lay surrounded by longish rye-grass not far from a beach. In the middle distance behind barbed wire fences stood a Russian bomber.

Susanne coughed again, a dry cough. She had just decided that her nose-bleed had been staunched sufficiently for her to let go of the tissue she were holding to it.

She lay back on her bed again, drawn and ivory, her hip bones and ribs almost protruding through her skin. She tilted her head back and lay back, her breathing slightly laboured.

A neighbour had visited her yesterday, someone from her block of flats whom she scarcely knew. Still it had been well meant.

Until the last few days, there had still been something of the ability to be daft in her, but now the shadow of exhaustion had extinguished it. She remembered *The Silly Sods Club*. 'You're the leader,' her friends had said.

Her husband had been a studious and decent man, thoughtful in his manner and highly proficient at mathematics and electrical engineering. Never really close – their love contrived, like second-rate actors on stage – he had always been respectful to her and not unkind. Yet she had felt relieved when he was out at work or she had to go on an errand. Her friend had said, 'If you are with the right one, it's not like that.' Their wedding had fallen on a saint's day and the priest had worn a red and gold stole. It had all looked so good, yet she had known it to be false.

The chaplain yesterday, had given her absolution.

In her remaining half-hour, she gasped heavily with her ravaged lungs and peered out of her clear sunken eyes.

She had not told Isolde of Lorenz, that strange man who had chased her all round Munich and written her the queerest but the only true love-letters she had ever had, because it might have upset her. It would have told her that she had not been born in love.

She had read a few lines by Bjørnson yesterday evening, just as her temperature reached its daily peak:

'No strength is left
To master thought or will;
Like scattered sheep bereft
They wander o'er the hill –
Ungathered, fading, drear:
For life's eclipse is near.'

And suddenly she thought that perhaps Lorenz would come to see her?

The ward clock said five past eleven. He saw her on her side gazing across the wide open floor between the two rows of beds, the light from a window silhouetting her wasted form.

He had removed his hat on entering the ward and shown his warrant to the very formal sister in charge. She had surveyed it critically before allowing him further.

He came round the end of her bed and stooped slightly.

She looked up and put her hand out a little. He moved his towards it. She touched his cuff as she had done all those years ago and smiled with a worn-out sweetness.

He knelt down.

Neither spoke for some time.

'Thank you for coming.'

He massaged the folds of loose skin on her neck and cheeks very gently with his knuckles.

'We women are strange creatures. We fight that which we most want.'

'Perhaps next time round we'll get it right ... if there is another time round?'

She nodded slowly. 'Please forgive me, Lorenz.'

'Of course.'

She raised her eyes and looked at his face.

He smiled.

'I'm sorry. I'm so terribly sorry.'

He unwrapped the painting of the *Scharnhorst* and held it up.

She breathed shallowly and rapidly and her eyes turned flickeringly upwards. 'I doubt they'll want that on the wall here.'

'Perhaps not.' He stroked her hair. 'Soon we shall be where foolish talk and incongruity do not exist.'

She continued to breathe erratically for another minute or two, then it faded and she died.

He went outside and as by some act of grace no one was around. He sat on a broken lump of concrete amid the dunes and looked at the gulls and the small waves lapping the beach and wept.

An hour later he started out on the path back to Ribnitz and the railway station, but he did not get far before he noted three men approaching.

It was his lot always to suffer and to struggle. But he had seen her and known at last that it was true … as if they had never been apart.

She had now left this knot of elusory happiness and temporal felicities and found an eternal peace.

But what awaited him? Oh well, no doubt he was about to find out. *Nemo ante mortem beatus* – no one is happy before death.

CHAPTER TWELVE

Spring had come to the Tirol.

Sitting on a rocky ledge, Uta looked out across the flat-bottomed valley. The scree-slope beside her tumbled down to a small blue lake with yellow reeds around it and a little beyond that the milky green river bubbled, its ripples glittering and twinkling in the sunshine. In the middle distance were the wide roofs of the scattered Alpine dwellings of the village and the needle-thin spire of the church. Green hummocks and pastures gradually rose up to the blue-tinged pine slopes which nestled below the sheer grey sides of mountains topped by their snowy peaks.

A man in waders and a battered hat stood in the river fly-fishing.

She ate her cheese and salami roll and sipped her bottle of milk.

For most of the day she wore a knee-length black dress with a tight laced-up bodice part and a white collar, a short white apron, white socks and black shoes with steel buckles. Together these constituted a simplified form of the traditional local costume. In this she served meals to the guests and cleared the tables in her cousin Emil's family-run Gasthof.

This cousin, who remembered her father for his brightening up pre-war family parties with games and tricks, had been very happy to offer Uta a temporary job, especially as the day before the West German police had rung, his daughter had suddenly announced her intention of going to live in Vienna.

The newcomer made a good impression on her relative, being cheerful and hard-working, though his wife Rosemarie remained tight-lipped, waiting perhaps for an excuse to criticise. Then two days ago, the daughter Andrea, who was younger than Uta, had unexpectedly returned. Not all young women have good legs, but Uta had. She looked prim and attractive and had just that right balance of coyness and approachability. Andrea hated her on sight.

Andrea had been working in a department store. She had enjoyed flirting, going to dances and cabarets and being dated ... until something had upset her.

Usually Uta took an afternoon walk. As she clambered down the rocks which led to a narrow foot-bridge suspended above a stream, a hearty voice hailed her.

'*Guten Tag, Fräulein.*' The fly-fisher waved but also beckoned. He waded up out of the water, put his rod down on the bank and came towards her. They met beside a tumbledown wooden cow-byre.

'Herr Dullenkopf?'

'I've been wanting to have a word with you,' puffed the dentist, who came from northern Germany and who was on holiday at the Gasthof.

'Indeed?'

'How do you like your job?'

She looked puzzled. 'It's all right.'

'Do you think you'll be here much longer, now that the host's charming daughter has come back?'

Now she understood. 'You're very observant.'

'I live near Hanover and I need a new receptionist.' A cow-bell clanged and they looked round at an approaching herd. 'Not as idyllic as here, but still pleasant.'

'Thank you,' she said with sincerity.

He watched her walk on towards the village. Had she been a western European, then pretty as she was she would have been more highly strung. In the East though, no one could take themselves too seriously, so happily she was mellower and more obliging.

Uta thought she could remain unperturbed by Andrea, but blood is thicker than water and already that evening impediments were being devised. The wife grew more demanding and abrasive. An old Scheitholt zither which hung on the wall in the Stübli was knocked and damaged by a guest and Uta found herself being blamed. Whilst being called *'ein dummes Mädchen'*, she saw Herr Dullenkopf grinning and shaking his head.

Whilst ordering a dessert he slipped her a note, which she tucked into her apron pocket.

A brash guest at the bar asked, 'When does the party start then?'

'When *she* leaves,' snarled Andrea, indicating Uta.

'Don't fall for Claus,' someone warned her. 'He only gives you half-litres.'

'Are we talking beer or sperm?' inquired Andrea with a dirty laugh.

Uta walked away.

At midnight in her cosy attic room, she read of Dullenkopf's offered post. The pearl glass bowl of the lamp emitted a yellow-white light which probed the cinerous corners of her tiny enclave. Receptionist-cum-surgery-assistant with a very fair wage and help in finding a flat. Dullenkopf seemed a decent enough fellow and besides, towns spelt opportunity. Emil had married into an Inn Valley family and so was prepared to tend goats, shovel snow and saw logs for winter, but to an outsider an Austrian village has little to offer.

Next to Uta's room was a large bathroom. Here she had had the luxury of a warm shower every morning. On the racks were piles of soap, shampoo and toothbrushes, which had at first astounded her by their contrast to the sparing and hand-to-mouth existence in the Eastern Zone.

Next morning she found Emil in the small smoke-house preparing to cure sausages and joints of bacon. She told him that she were leaving and he nodded. 'I'm sorry it's ended like this, but it's been nice having you.'

She walked back across the yard to the chalet of white-washed stone and roughly-hewn wood with its carved balconies, geraniums and Biblical quotes in Gothic lettering.

Two days later she boarded the yellow post-bus.

*   *   *   *

The numbers 251266 had been tattooed onto Bauss's right forearm.

Eight hundred convicts were working on a nuclear bunker.

The sun, like a thin pancake, had settled low on the horizon and a worn and grey-looking Lorenz leant on his shovel.

The steam excavator had broken down and this gang were shovelling heavy reddish clay into a dumper truck.

He soldiered on, but his ageing frame – unused to such

exertion – could scarcely stand it.

But, time for the evening meal. He trudged after the others, across a gouged out hillside in the failing light.

Beyond the wide expanse of the airfield, in the russet-streaked rock hill, tunnels for fighter aircraft and missiles were being blasted.

They ate their bowls of potato, turnip and water with salt and an occasional shred of meat, seated on benches beneath draped camouflage nets made of rope with strips of green and brown jute woven loosely into them.

Two moujiks watched them, Russian peasants looking for an excuse to wield the knout.

On his pallet in the camp that night, Lorenz dreamt he were offering a raisin cake to a Nordic priestess. She placed a hand firmly on his head. Our shortcomings make tragedies inevitable.

*　　　*　　　*　　　*

Herr Dullenkopf lived in Celle, a North German town whose wedge-shaped main square had many medieval-looking buildings; some original, some new.

In Westcelletorstrasse Uta took a flat above a baker's with the rather twee name of 'Lottchens Backstube'. Her abode was tiny but modern.

The dentist's suite would have made its East German equivalent seem like a museum; immaculately clean, bright floor-tiles, green plastic-coated doors and the fittings were all so simple neat and exact.

She answered the telephone, booked appointments, cleaned sets of oral probes and mirrors, sterilised the instruments and made the coffee.

After a few weeks, Herr Dullenkopf asked if she would baby-sit for him.

At his post-war house, his wife was speaking on the telephone, ordering flowers. 'What colour? Er ... they're for a friend in Monastir, so ... What colour? She's an interior designer, so ... What colour? Sort of bold ... '

Frau Dullenkopf wore trousers, which then were still a little progressive. She also seemed decidedly up-herself and exhibited showy airs.

With the parents gone, Uta found herself in a modishly furnished sitting-room with twelve-year-old twins. The girl had been to the cinema that afternoon.

'What was the film?' Uta asked.

It had been some American romance.

'Boyfriends,' explained the boy.

'You can rely on your brother to drop you in it, can't you?'

The girl shrugged and thumbed a magazine.

The boy scoffed chocolate and switched on their new television. An advert described the dilemma of buying a new car; stylish with creature comforts or aggressive and macho? Well now you could have both.

What rubbish. No wonder these kids had such limited imaginations.

She made herself coffee and went to the window, to watch the rain trickling down the glass and the birds seeking refuge beneath the foliage.

In the town, bright chic ski-jackets were the latest craze. West Germans had become very cosmopolitan; foreigners almost who just happened to have German ancestry.

Next day at work, in her medium-blue short-sleeved dress and yellow nylon tabard, she caught her boss looking at her calves. A painting on the waiting-room wall was entitled 'Brumaire' and portrayed a foggy day at Rouen market. Herr Dullenkopf explained – whilst resting a hand lightly on her shoulder – that during the French revolution, November had been renamed 'Brumaire', the 'month of fog'.

During their afternoon coffee break, he said, 'I'm sorry if my wife gave a rather bad impression last night.'

Uta rocked her head from side to side non-committally.

'You only saw the tip of the iceberg.

One of her favourite pastimes is wrecking social encounters. The dog eats a pretzel say? Although there are dozens of them, she will have a tantrum and when she has ruined everyone's evening, smile.'

'Ought you to tell me this?'

'I've been loyal for years … but suddenly I don't care. I wish to tell someone … someone with understanding.'

Uta had an uneasy feeling. 'But I cannot advise you, Herr Dullenkopf.'

'Wolfram, please … and it is still consoling even if someone simply listens.'

'But it's only a palliative.'

Uta rinsed their cups in the sink.

'There is another half of this story.'

She thought, 'Oh no. Here it comes.'

He reached out for her hand. She retracted her arm with a jerk and knocked the milk over. She picked up a floor-cloth and bent down, but he seized her wrists.

'You're imagining things.'

By now they were both kneeling.

He had thought of her when in bed. When he lay on top of his wife, he imagined she were Uta.

She fought only hard enough to prevent him from doing anything unseemly.

He offered her marriage and she did for an instant – but only for an instant – hesitate. Her life was after all rather lonely, but she quickly rallied.

His assistant came in and put her hand to her mouth.

Uta knew she had to find another job.

*   *   *   *

Christoph took a job folding boxes in a warehouse in Mannheim.

Early one evening, in his rabbit-hutch flat in a part of the city called the Oststadt, he sat reading the play, *The Fair Druidess*.

In act one, some travellers, stranded on an island with an enchanted temple, find that it is only possible to speak the truth. The boastful or conceited are lessened, whilst conversely the merits of the shy or the thoughtful are more evident. This though soon palls and without a seasoning of half-truths and bluff, coexistence becomes fraught.

He broke off.

Suddenly he felt lonely. He had lost his father and his sister, whilst his mother and his only close friend were stuck in the East.

He went out to *Das Eismeer*, a Bierkeller, where the lads from the warehouse often went for a drink, but only Hans the fork-lift driver was there, carousing with a curly-haired girl, so no one even to play table-football with.

He eavesdropped on an English couple.

'I'm an ornithologist,' she said.

'What does that mean?'

'It means I like nightjars and blue-tits.'

'So a drink in the evening and hypothermic breasts?'

Christoph could not follow.

A girl wearing a long jangly neck-chain and a puffy-sleeved dress started to play an accordion.

He walked down to the River Neckar, where large river barges were moored. He passed a café with an outdoor terrace where groups laughed and chatted beneath fake vine leaves.

Near the Luisenpark, an A-board on the pavement advertised a free concert and an arrow indicated a squat inconspicuous church.

The interior was rectangular, with balconies on three sides and a little dreary. The modest audience was spread out thinly and Christoph sat to one side and towards the back. The instrumentalists were tuning up.

They began with a Brahms piano and 'cello sonata, treacly and lacking in melody. He was beginning to feel bored, when he noted the other occupant of his hard vertically-backed pew.

She sat quite calmly well away from him, yet he thought he sensed – as one does – a subtle sexual magnetism.

She occasionally crossed her legs or looked at her programme. Despite her seeming concentration on the performance, he knew that she was as aware of him as he was of her. She did not turn to look at him though, for he watched her out of the corner of his eye.

Five years older than himself he guessed, neat and feminine in form with soft shoulder-length fair hair. Her face was a little plain and care-worn and it had a few spots. Her dress was simple but tasteful – black tights and pointed black shoes, a navy skirt, a three-quarter jacket, silver ear-rings and minimal if any make-up. Her navy leather handbag again was plain yet expensive and lay on the seat beside her.

Her invisible Gaussian lines of attraction were just the tonic he needed.

Could she be the wife of an architect or a lawyer who had run off with his secretary? Even with a good figure and education and means, life might not be easy for her. Men of the right age would mostly be either spoken for or also have messy relationships behind them.

Christoph imagined that he felt sorry for her and saw himself comforting her. This was perhaps the sort of girl he needed?

A Russian pianist hammered the keys bordering on the fanatical. The 'cellist was inaudible.

Christoph wore a grey anorak of stiffish cotton, black trousers and shoes and a clean orange shirt. By good fortune he looked reasonably well turned out.

A lively Brandenburg concerto caused him to refocus some of his attention on the musicians. His neighbour gave him a brief indeterminate glance.

In the interval, at the rear of the church, he bought a cup of coffee and a finger of apple-cake. The other listeners gathered in groups and chatted, as they mostly knew one another. The elegant girl though took a lonely stroll and stopped beside a selection of pamphlets. She also it seemed, was not a part of the local musical scene.

Christoph felt an optimistic warmth suffuse his body, a mix of desire and affection, of lust and egoism and he set course to woo or seduce this mystery girl.

'Good evening. Are you enjoying the concert?' It was the obvious opener and suitably non-committal.

She turned and smiled slightly, leaning her head to one side. 'I liked the Bach.'

'Likewise.'

Isolde had once said, 'Brahms would often be better with two or three less voices – or lines – in the score. It's overly rich.'

The girl grinned indulgently, though in a detached rather than an encouraging way. It could be read as, 'I'm entertained by your flirting with me,' or 'We're not children, just say what you want.' To try to distinguish between these, he asked, 'Do you often go to concerts by yourself?'

Her acne-spotted face emitted a rather rigid stare which somehow hinted that she was harder or more indifferent than he had guessed. 'Sometimes.'

That had unveiled nothing. Her manner was not flirtatious yet neither was it definitely cool or stand-offish. To solve the enigma, he chose the ruse of drifting off to see if she would make a move, but she did not.

A bell sounded for the second half. Taking the bull by the horns, Christoph sat down right beside her, as if they were together. He felt pretty desperate, so why not be bold? He had nothing to lose. No one there knew him.

She stayed perfectly still.

Christoph was neither lecherous nor sex-obsessed,

just lonely. He wanted company, love, affection, a warm female to cuddle and kiss and drink coffee with. He felt in her aura, a light if unseen electro-static bond. He tentatively moved a hand to hold hers, which rested in her lap. Without a movement on her face, her warm thin sex-promising fingers received his. His breast trembled slightly.

He wanted her. He wanted her suddenly so much.

She lived in an elegant top-floor flat a few blocks away, with a large picture window which overlooked the broad green park and beyond it the river and the parallel canal.

They sat on the long low sofa and consumed coffee with walnut cake and chocolates and half-listened to music with initially barely a word spoken.

Only when he slid an arm round her appealingly delicate shoulders and the lingeringly pleasant foretastes of love began, did she start to talk on and off in a quiet tone.

'Do you work ... or have a career?'

'I've been folding boxes for a month. That's not a career.'

She smiled. 'A career is a job which has gone on for too long. I've recently divorced.'

'I'm sorry.'

'Don't be. My husband was a top chef ... his late nights made life difficult.'

There would be more to it than that, thought Christoph. 'Were his omelettes not up to scratch? Or his meat balls?'

She ignored this.

He fingered her breasts. 'I worked on the railways ... in East Germany.'

She required discreet titillation and physical relief, he

sensed, but away from her usual circle of associates.

'I teach Italian.'

'Here?'

'In Heidelberg.'

He stroked the left one spirally, turning it into a hazel-nut whirl. He undid her blouse and kissed her forcefully on her lips.

She stood up, took his hand and led him through to the bedroom.

She dropped her skirt and her panties.

As a long and active night got underway, he learnt that her name was Liese Hoh, that she had no children, a deep unsatisfied love-void and had become fairly cynical of a hard world.

Christoph's convivial innocence proved to be an advantage. Liese's husband had been a chimera, hiding some unconfessed perversity. After their first month, she knew he was totally untrustworthy.

Sex both perplexed and pleased Liese. At times during an exhausting three hours, she quaked as she yielded to her own half-suppressed needs.

Daylight found him face-down, half beneath her and with one leg between hers.

She awoke serenely and dreamily stroked his stubbly hair.

'How is my sweet donkey today?'

'Relaxed and contented. His last girlfriend was unkind … '

'Perhaps we should report her to the Office for Animal Cruelty?'

In contrast to Greta, Liese had the sense and the talents

to be both tender and imaginative.

It was Sunday morning.

After breakfast, they took a trip in her car.

By pure luck, they saw a hot-air balloon in a field and they just made up the numbers for a flight.

After two weeks of seeing one another, she asked out of the blue, 'Do you think we're meant to be together?'

He nodded.

'We'll go and visit my parents in Duisburg. I'll wear a different blouse. Last time I saw my mother, she unbraided me about a U-shaped neck-line which showed the top of my cleavage.'

*   *   *   *

Cowl-shaped clouds hung ominously over Hanover as Uta arrived for her interview with the solicitors.

She had on a new bright-red raincoat and her well-polished black leather boots, which with her long dark plait made her look striking though perhaps unsophisticated. The other two interviewees were dressed in smarter, tweedy, more office-like attire.

The three interviewers wore expensive suits and were quietly confident of their success and position. In East Germany one met brutal selfishness, in West Germany it was suave and well-schooled selfishness.

Two legal terms which she did not understand, quickly cropped up. After an awkward pause, the senior partner said, 'Well, I think we're through here, Fräulein Dietl.'

On the train back to Celle, she looked out at the rain falling on the fields of beet and barley and the copses dotting the flat landscape.

At a farming hamlet, an old fellow in long socks and hunting breeches boarded.

Eyeing her with a twinkle, he said, 'Cheer up.'

She smiled. 'I've just fluffed an interview.'

'As what?'

'A solicitor's receptionist.'

'Well … probably a lucky escape?'

The train was passing through woodland. The trees were well-spaced and the forest floor displayed broad swaths of wild flowers, blue and pink. '*So rief der Lenz in den Wald,*' the old man quoted Wagner. 'Thus spring echoed through the forest.'

A bird – perhaps a ptarmigan – flew alongside.

'Where are you from?'

'Thuringia.'

'East Germany?'

'Yes. I escaped.'

'In the war we feared being captured by the Russians. My unit was in the Caucasus – trying to break through to the Persian and Iraqi oilfields – when we were encircled. I developed wet beriberi and my body swelled up.' His hands depicted its bloated size. 'This M.O. from Kazan gave me a box of vitamin B pills and said, "Eat the lot," so I did. An hour later I needed a wee. I was just coming out when I wanted to go again and then a third time. So I decided to stay there for an hour just weeing on and off till I'd lost all this water. A good fellow. I recall him in my prayers now and then.'

The train whistled piercingly as it rattled over a barriered level-crossing where a tractor with a draw-bar trailer full of turnips waited.

'Do you need a job?'

'Yes.'

He liked the character of his travelling companion. 'My son runs a catering business. He's short-handed. Write your name and address down.'

He fumbled in his pockets, but she found the interview letter in her handbag. 'Here.'

Three days later, near Bad Fallingbostel, Uta with a dozen others in black skirts or trousers and white blouses or shirts, arrived to serve food and drink in a huge marquee.

The 'event' was an open day involving both the *Bundeswehr* and the British Army; display teams, side-shows, rides on vehicles, a demonstration of bridging equipment, brass bands and so on. It was a bank holiday; warm sunny and cloudless.

A grassy field had been cordoned off and at the wide visitors' entrance on the perimeter, stood a tank-transporter trailer with welcome hoardings on it and two British Redcaps.

When a bus dropped the caterers off early in the day, one of these Provos smiled at Uta.

Inside the huge tent she had the task of pouring out aliquots of lemonade into plastic beakers for the children to glug. Beside her were the coffee squad and beyond them the buns and easy meals contingents.

She remembered the urbane, smart and smiling sergeant who had greeted them at the entrance to the base.

An Italian in the coffee team, plied her with awful chat-up lines, but her eyebrows said, 'Please, just buzz off.'

Outside, Sergeant Eiros Jones conversed with Woody,

his colleague. 'There's Colonel Godwin's wife, Lady Godiva.'

'Yes … a woman who wears the trousers.'

'Figuratively yes, but historically not.'

'Anyway, soon time for us to be relieved. And I just fancy some refreshments from that there tent.'

A German civilian approached the military policemen. 'Sumvun az stohlen mine vollet.'

Woody muttered, 'Say you think it's that waitress lass … it'll give you an excuse to go and see her.'

Jones said, 'I'm sorry to hear that, Sir. How do you think it happened?'

Eiros was Welsh, solid and energetic, though not particularly tall. Behind his practised military frown, he was both genial and honest.

In East Germany Uta had been regarded as a touch too informal, whilst in West Germany people saw her as quite stiff.

She stooped to tidy away some used tumblers into a crate, before righting herself to dispense more lemonade to a waiting queue of boys, girls and a sergeant. Her heart missed a beat, but she dissembled.

When it was his turn, he handed her the required four Pfennigs and said in a clipped way, 'A glass of lemonade, please Miss.'

The circumstances enabled her to understand this. Outside a band was playing a lively quick march.

'It's called *The Keel Row*,' he said, having noted her prick up her ears.

She nodded and smiled, though it meant nothing to her.

'Excuse me Miss, but may I ask your name?'

Name? She knew that word. 'Uta,' she said, trying hard not to blush, 'Not pretty?'

'Well … but you are.'

She could not reply to this.

'Thank you for the lemonade.' He moved off and the space was immediately filled by a cluster of small jostling bodies. She spilt some of the liquid from the next bottle, as her hands shook with that tremulous excitement that is almost fear.

She had made no mistake. When later the caterers were packing up, there he was, courteously being helpful. This time he had the courage to use his limited German or perhaps he had used the interval to brush up on it. *'Guten Tag, noch einmal.'*

She maintained something of a detached demeanour.

'Could I ask you out tomorrow afternoon?' he whispered with fierce seriousness.

She looked at him curiously.

'A trip to Rodmansheide?' He looked at her intensely. 'Where do you live?'

'Celle.'

'If I met you in the French Garden? One o'clock?'

She smiled puckishly and held up a forefinger. 'One o'clock,' was all she could manage.

Back in her flat that evening, she felt bemused. Was it sensual anticipation? Not at all. It was something quite different – hope yes, but also a sort of inexplicable ecstasy.

*   *   *   *

At the construction site the prisoners were shovelling hard-core.

Lorenz felt a pain in his chest and looked ill. He was allowed to sit for a while. He looked out over the shallows of a weed-filled canal. By the farther bank, lay a sunken barge.

A tunnel collapse had been blamed on the German civil engineer. Concrete able to withstand a compression force of only two hundred kilograms per square centimetre – as tested on a poured sample block – had been used instead of the design-required four hundred and with vibration and compaction not adequately overseen. A shortage of heavier reinforcing rods and of cement with a higher alumina content meant that compromises had been necessary, but no one mentioned that at the inquiry.

Bauss's chest pain spread up into his throat. He unbuckled his belt.

He heard the shot. 'So, Dieter's beaten me to it.'

But did any of this matter? Susanne had confessed that she had always known he was the right one. He had been vindicated at last. All true love is madness. It is unique and can never be counterfeited.

His heart made some queer somersaults and he said, 'This is it. Now I am going.'

*   *   *   *

Eiros rode up on a motorcycle.

They went to a small quiet lake edged by a crop of green corn.

One single oak, cleft down the middle by a fork of lightning had sprouted new green buds in spite of its bare wounds. Its charred hollow showed that children lit fires in its split bole, which by killing the mould and fungi might have enabled it to survive.

Round its base grew a cluster of blue and pink phlox.

Sitting on Uta's red nylon raincoat, they watched the ducks and ate a small picnic which she had brought and which he had stowed in his bike's panniers.

Uta had not made love before, but only heard of how delightful it was. Falling in love had yet to become unfashionable or unnecessary.

After two hours the mellow ochre sun waned, its ball of dripping honey masked by feathered clouds, the mournful grey-red dappled heralds of evening.

It started to rain. On the flower-dotted bank beside them, the blue cornflowers hung their heads and gusts of sharp droplets sent waves through the corn.

These were not yet the days of free love. The young were not afraid of joy, yet would usually govern their lusts. They had come through the war and they knew that many who were better than they had died. They kept smiling in their honour. You did not sleep with your boyfriend until you knew you would marry him.

They sailed to Britain for their honeymoon from the quay at Rendsburg on the Kiel Canal, on the cargo-boat *Axenfels*. Even the North Sea looked summery – greeny-blue with gold dust on the bottom – and the sky so calm and clear.

She would always remember these happy days. No detail was mean or unimportant.

*   *   *   *

247

Six months earlier Nurse Spitz had been ushered in to Balthasar Axt at the *Grenzpolizei* H.Q.

He concurred with Bauss in his appreciation of her body's contours. If at first glance though, she appeared quite chaste, a closer scrutiny suggested hidden impurities. Such is life. Nothing is perfect; always a sting in the tail.

'Your physique Heidi, seemingly tantalised Herr Bauss?'

She seemed quite proud of it.

'What if I too am drawn?'

She gave him a sly smile.

The interrogation was perfunctory as she knew nothing.

'You have understanding ... ' he mused, 'not shallow like so many young lasses.'

'Is that a compliment?'

'A provisional one. You have to live up to it of course '

She smiled uncertainly.

By unspoken intimation though, she rekindled that youthful passion in him, to just ravish a sexy girl.

He fixed her up in a flat above the Café Potemkin, near the Friedrichstrasse Station in Berlin.

Heidi had to comply with his demands, share her body's latent delights and restrain her abrasive ways.

Axt was mercenary and detested fake talk. He avoided the word 'love' like the plague.

He had given up on the search for the gold, contenting himself with the icing – and not the cake – which was his new mistress; she who Phoenix-like had risen from the ashes of that venture.

In the spring, they took a short holiday at his mountain retreat.

Swishing through an unmown pasture, with the echoes

248

of a cuckoo's two-tone call sounding down in the valley, she said that she wished to return to Thuringia.

He stopped. 'Do you know something?'

The President had been quite cool with him lately.

'The midges only pester you. They must like your sweat.'

'Who's spoken to you?'

She hesitated. 'Elena Eletskaya, I think her name was.'

'Oh. She drove a T34 tank in the war.' A pity they had not succeeded in blowing it up.

'She asked about foreign bank accounts … but I didn't know anything.'

Sweat moistened his back.

In her youth, Elena had fancied herself as *une Vénus moscovite*, but later, on becoming coarse and tubby, had turned to politics.

Three days later Axt vanished and Heidi went back to Essbach.

EPILOGUE

Eiros and Uta settled near Abergavenny, where he ran a cycle shop called *The Lightstrung* and she worked part-time in the bookshop. They had two sons.

The English language came quite easily to her. She learnt a little Welsh too.

On a holiday in Northumberland she sent a picture postcard of furry white chicks on a sandy beach to her handicapped nephew Iddo. She had no idea whether it would be delivered.

Later they bought Goosegog Farm near Caer Suus, a run-down stone house whose neighbour's sheep kept getting through the fence and eating their grass.

Uta sometimes cleaned Eiros's motorcycle as Andromache had fed hay to Hector's horse. The couple were kind to one another or if occasionally not, they would say sorry and ask for forgiveness. With her boys too she took a genuine interest in their hobbies.

In Cynfor's school physics book, she read of the Leclanché cell. 'Due to its rapid polarisation, it is not good for constant current supply but rather for intermittent usage.' The telephone at Aunt Monika's had had this type of cell.

One morning, whilst hanging the clothes out on a line between the two apple trees, she heard Cynfor practising his violin – for which he had little talent – and recollected Isolde. No totalitarian rule can ever eradicate that unspoken Freemasonry of honesty and good-will between good people.

Observing the shallow valley's woods and knolls, she remembered the old saw, that it is not the land which belongs to you, but you who belong to the land. We only exist as a part of something larger than ourselves.

Eiros was baling hay.

On a bone-shaking old single-decker she went into Newtown to pay some bills. In a café near the Victorian infants' school with its cobbled yard and green-painted iron railings, she bought tea and cheese on toast.

Out of the blue an older man eyed her. Eventually he leant over and whispered, 'Is it Uta?'

'Yes,' she answered.

'Terenz. Rohrdorf signal-box.'

'Good gracious. What are you doing here?'

'Visiting. I live in Shrewsbury.'

'So you escaped too?'

'There was a special train which I knew would not be searched, so I crept aboard.

'What about the signal-box?'

'Someone else was on duty.

When you and Christoph escaped, I heard the shots and wondered whether to hold the train … but decided not to get involved.'

'How did you know who it was?'

'I didn't, not until a few days later. At least that bastard who hit you was dead.'

'You must come and visit us … but please don't mention the shooting.'

*   *   *   *

For two years Christoph and Liese rubbed along well enough. They travelled and had no children, but Liese drank a lot.

When she leant against a pillar with her body in an S-bend, a provocative stare and rouge-tinged lips, she could still be mildly exciting.

After watching a perfect performance of *Uncle Vanya* – so profound yet down to earth – he burnt six of his nine half-written plays, like the first six of the nine Sibylline Books.

He then discovered that Liese was having an affair with a young pop guitarist whom they knew and whom he referred to as 'Banjo Joe'.

In the Italian resort of Viareggio, under a white and blue sunshade, he watched girls in bikinis bathing on the beach. The sea had a film on its surface of sun-tan lotion.

At an outdoor café, backed by shrubs, he sipped a *café au lait* and ate a segmented Valencia orange with cream. A girl appeared and smiled. '*Ich heisse* Concetta. *Komm mit.*' She led him to a dark quiet room where apart from the sand blown in from the beach on its marble floor, there was only a bed.

Concetta was black haired and sallow skinned and though only sixteen, could well simulate a lascivious affection.

The girls of his childhood were not so much naïve as inexperienced. They wanted what was orderly and aimed for stable married lives. They were not over-inhibited, but wary of flattery and willing to wait … at least for a time.

Concetta said, 'Well, do you want me?'

What would Egeria have said to King Numa?

God had occupied a much more immediate place in his sister's mind. She might be making soup or ironing a blouse, but it was always a step removed from the centre of her being.

Events had seemed transient and ephemeral to them then; not as solid and certain as today's surroundings.

He walked out.

*   *   *   *

After the dissolution of the Communist regime, Uta visited a transformed Essbach.

Her hair was now greying, but she was still slender and able-bodied.

It was a calm summer's day as she walked out of the railway station onto new pavements and passed brightly filled shop windows and open-air cafés. She too had been modernised; white leather sandals, a blue and white patterned frock and a matt blue Gortex jacket. Gone were the belted raincoats and the knitted stockings of her youth.

The *Grenzpolizei* Headquarters had become the head office of a large communications company with a flashing orange quincuncial logo on a metal-framed tower on the grass in front of it and the gas works had been replaced by a supermarket. She bought some flowers and walked to the cemetery and the grave of her grandfather.

By chance she saw too that of Isolde, covered in rough grass and white hellebores. A small headstone had been placed there by the church.

Isolde Elisabeth Lyskirchen

1931 - 1955

Ehre sei Gott in der Höhe

On the town's southern perimeter shoddy grey three-storey

flats had been built in the sixties. No informants lurked there now, yet a kind of sinister aura hung over them.

She walked out past Edstedt where she had lugged her kitbag that fateful evening in 1955 and on the hump-backed bridge looked down at the railway. They were laying new track and electric colour-light signals were replacing the old semaphore ones. Onto piles of bright white ballast a hydraulic crane was placing new lengths of track with concrete sleepers.

She carried on into the wood and took the baked-earth track which led to the quarry. The spur of track there had gone and the trees been cut back. A gang were busy dismantling the old signal against which she had leant when feeling faint after Joos had punched her.

Its post was not of the usual lattice-girder type, but a square hollow girder made out of four plates riveted to four outwardly-facing angle girders, forming a hollow 'H' section. It was topped by an ornate finial. The signal arm was a bar with a circle on the end, white but edged in red.

As the oxy-acetylene torch burnt its way into the fifty-centimetre broad post, the operator made an inaudible comment. When it tumbled, inside it were large black brick-like lumps. One of these had been cut and partly melted by the flame-cutter. The men stood and gaped. '*Es ist das Gold!*'

In 1944 Stehr had climbed up the fixed ladder, removed the finial and carried the ingots up one at a time and dropped them into it, but thirty-nine had filled it to the top.

Back in the town, Uta ate lunch at an Italian restaurant. She wanted to say, 'I come from here. This is my town,' but it was not so any more.

The foreigner who served her dropped the fork as he

brought her spaghetti and she bent forwards to pick it up. Did he know that that meant a woman would visit him?

After her meal, she had had enough. She wanted to be back on Goosegog Farm.

And when she arrived home, she dug out an old photograph. It showed her in her *Grenzpolizei* uniform, the plain blue tilted Glengarry-type cap with its badge, the leather coat and boots, the holster with its pistol and the truncheon. It was of course black and white and whether or not it was the photography she could not say, but it seemed like dusk. Behind her a rough masonry wall with icicles dangling from its coping stones also hinted at a rather bleak world.

Eiros sat beside her and viewed the picture. 'If it were not for your sweet face, that would look quite sinister.'

'True, but we never saw it like that.'

*   *   *   *

In Essbach, Luise and Torsten remained together. He continued to teach at the University and they had two children.

Their garden backed onto a twinkling chrome-flecked stream, edged with larkspur and here in a summerhouse he studied old or obscure books. Some from the library – relegated to the stacks – the old librarian would give him. 'Keep it. No one else will ever read it.'

Luise was happy to escape the terrible parties of her communist bosses in East Berlin, where status was indicated not by glittering dresses or attractive uniforms, but by the degree of servility exhibited in those around these suited nonentities.

Niehaus married Viktoria and also became a virger at

the Johanneskirche and so frequently saw the organ's long polished stool, its round ebony stops – *Clarion ottavino* and *Fagott, Geigen* and *Prinzipal Gedeckt* – and the rows of pipes, oak for flute-toned stops, zinc for the bass ones and tin and lead alloy to give a bright sound for the oboe and trumpet ranks.

The pastoral angel painted on wood – whom fortunately no one has been insensitive enough to restore – still looks down and smiles when the sun from the high clerestory windows falls onto her face.

*　　*　　*　　*

So trusty reader, you who have stayed the course, here I am again, the Genius of the Locus.

Life's unexpected twists need not be feared by the good or the true.

Uta had subconsciously known – even in her youth – that change and chance would come her way; that life would open out.

Lorenz's bruised and cut heart was finally healed and as to the gold – which did exist – it was not given to anyone in this story.

When I go, this line of priestesses will end. I am the last of the strange maid-servants of the old gods; but that too is as it is meant to be.

Loosestrife – a marsh plant – has started to grow in the wet ground around the base of my sacred slanting rock and around the stump of the old signal post.

THE END.